D0524337

Bryn knew, with fierce certainty, that his dad's death had not been the result of a 'freak accident at work'. . . Somebody had deliberately and cold-bloodedly arranged his death. Bryn was determined to find out who had killed him and why.

Bryn has never bothered much about politics and how the world is run. After all, it is the end of the twenty-second century, and the world is at peace, ruled by the President and the global companies. But when his dad dies in mysterious circumstances in his laboratory at Globechem, Bryn begins to ask questions.

And Bryn is not the only one to question the way things are: Jade has always felt an outsider, able to see and feel things other people can't and plagued by a sense of foreboding and apocalyptic visions. When she and Bryn get together, they realize that perhaps things are not always what they seem, that the world may not be perfect after all . . . and that they are in terrible danger.

Carol Hedges was born in Hertfordshire and after university, where she gained a BA(Hons) in English Literature, she trained as a children's librarian. She has had various jobs including running her own children's clothes business, being a se   , a dinner lady, and a   assistant at a special needs school. Later she retrained as   teacher. In 1999 she gave up full time work to concentrate on her writing. She has had several books published and a short story broadcast on the radio. *Bright Angel* is her third novel for Oxford University Press.

Bright Angel

Carol Hedges

OXFORD
UNIVERSITY PRESS

For Ron, with thanks and respect

OXFORD
UNIVERSITY PRESS

Great Clarendon Street, Oxford OX2 6DP

Oxford University Press is a department of the University of Oxford.
It furthers the University's objective of excellence in research, scholarship,
and education by publishing worldwide in

Oxford New York

Athens Auckland Bangkok Bogotá Buenos Aires
Cape Town Chennai Dar es Salaam Delhi Florence Hong Kong Istanbul
Karachi Kolkata Kuala Lumpur Madrid Melbourne Mexico City Mumbai
Nairobi Paris São Paulo Shanghai Singapore Taipei Tokyo Toronto Warsaw
and associated companies in Berlin Ibadan

Oxford is a registered trade mark of Oxford University Press
in the UK and in certain other countries

Copyright © Carol Hedges 2002

The moral rights of the author have been asserted

Database right Oxford University Press (maker)

First published 2002

All rights reserved. No part of this publication may be reproduced,
stored in a retrieval system, or transmitted, in any form or by any means,
without the prior permission in writing of Oxford University Press.
Within the UK, exceptions are allowed in respect of any fair
dealing for the purpose of research or private study, or criticism or
review, as permitted under the Copyright, Designs and Patents Act 1988,
or in the case of reprographic reproduction in accordance with
the terms of the licences issued by the Copyright Licensing Agency.
Enquiries concerning reproduction outside these terms and in other
countries should be sent to the Rights Department, Oxford University Press,
at the above address.

This book is sold subject to the condition that it shall not, by way of trade or
otherwise, be lent, re-sold, hired out or otherwise circulated without
the publisher's prior consent in any form of binding or cover other than that in
which it is published and without a similar condition including this condition
being imposed on the subsequent purchaser.

British Library Cataloguing in Publication Data available

ISBN 0 19 271898 3

1 3 5 7 9 10 8 6 4 2

Typeset by AFS Image Setters Ltd, Glasgow
Printed in Great Britain

20070602

MORAY COUNCIL
LIBRARIES &
INFORMATION SERVICES

JCY

I am Alpha and Omega, the beginning and the end, the first and the last.

Revelation 22:13

Alpha

'Silly question . . . '

'Yeah, go on.'

'Why are you doing this?'

Bryn dropped a spadeful of earth into the bucket. 'Geography project,' he said shortly. He didn't look up. He dug the spade in the earth again, shovelled some more into the bucket.

'Geography project?' Gil frowned. 'We gave that in last week.'

'Biology, then.'

'Respiration in mammals?'

'Yeah, that.'

'Respiration,' Gil repeated the words slowly and emphatically, 'in . . . mammals. You don't have to dig a hole. Specially a big one.'

Bryn stopped digging, looked around him. Gil was right. Dead right. It was a big hole, as holes went. And as holes went, it was going well. The hole is always equal to the sum of its parts, he thought. Some of its parts were boredom, anger, and frustration. Nothing to do, nowhere to go. The not-allowed-outness was getting to him big time. The hole, started last week to get soil samples for a school experiment, had become an outlet for his pent-up feelings. A way of two-fingering the system: if he couldn't go out, he would go down. Nobody could stop him doing that. Could they?

'Man, you are crazy, you know that.' Gil shook his head sadly.

1

'Maybe . . . '

'What'll your mum say when she sees this?'

'Nothing,' Bryn resumed digging, 'because she won't see it.'

Not in a million years, he thought. She never came out into the garden. Not since his dad had gone. He'd been the gardener. And the rest. Always pottering around after work. Therapy, he'd called it, getting in touch with his roots. His mum had little interest in the garden then. None whatsoever now.

That was the other reason for digging the hole: the great gaping void in his heart that couldn't be put into words. A sadness so vast and deep that the only thing he could do to block it out was exhaust himself. When it first hit him, the pain of loss, he'd gone running. He ran miles, head down, his breath ripping out in rags, feet pounding the unforgiving streets. Until the night he was picked up by the police at two in the morning running round the perimeter fence outside his dad's work. Now he was grounded. Temporarily. So the only way to tire himself out was to dig. Maybe it was stupid. Maybe Gil was right. But at least he slept nights.

Right now, the summer afternoon was at its height. Before too long the sun would begin to sink westward into a pink and golden sky. A little breeze cooled Bryn's face, ruffled Gil's fair hair as he stared down into the hole.

'You going to be much longer?' he asked.

Bryn attached the bucket to the makeshift rope pulley. 'Haul away,' he commanded. Gil pulled up the bucket, tipped the earth out and sent it back down. It was better with Gil there, Bryn thought. Before, he had to shift the earth himself.

'Only I think I should be getting back.' Gil frowned. 'I promised I would be back straight after school.'

'Yeah, right. You go.' Bryn nodded. That was Gil, he

2

thought. No trouble to anybody. Always the good guy. He put down the spade, clambered out of the hole. They were so different, he thought. Sometimes he wondered how the two of them had managed to remain friends for so long.

Together, the two boys walked back towards the house.

'So . . . what've you got planned for tonight?' Gil asked.

'Don't know. Bit of schoolwork. Play on my computer. Watch TV.' Bryn deliberately kept his voice vague. 'You?'

'Same,' Gil replied. 'See you tomorrow then.'

'Yeah. See you.'

From the top of the garden, you couldn't see the hole. It was masked by the big brick-sided shed. His dad's shed. Bryn stood staring at the shed, remembering. His dad barking orders for tools, himself scurrying round collecting them. The two of them bent over the workbench. His dad's hands delicately probing with a tiny silver screwdriver; lifting out tiny circuit boards and putting them back. Like a surgeon performing an intricately complex operation. Both of them totally focused, concentrated. The silence so sharp you could cut yourself on it. Bryn felt a familiar pain, like pressing upon an unhealed bruise. The bruise of loss. It hadn't healed. He knew it never would. Not until he understood clearly exactly what had gone wrong.

Darya, Bryn's eight-year-old sister, was sitting on the couch in the family room. Her face lit up when she saw him come in.

'Hi, Bryn!' she yelled. 'Can I come upstairs and play in your room?'

Bryn looked down at her. 'Sorry, Da,' he said, 'I've got to study. Big test tomorrow.'

Darya's small face fell. 'But it's *Tuesday*,' she protested, 'you always have tests on Friday!'

'Tomorrow's the big exception.' Bryn lied fluently. 'Later maybe.'

Darya pulled a face. 'What's for dinner?' she asked.

'Something.'

'Something what?'

'Something meat with something veggies and chips followed by something pudding and I scream.'

Darya grinned delightedly. This was a game they'd played since as far back as both of them could remember. She still enjoyed it. Bryn had kind of lost the thrill years ago.

'Come and watch some TV with me?' she asked, wriggling up on the couch and patting the space next to her invitingly. Bryn groaned inwardly. Darya looked up at him, big blue eyes wide with hope. 'Please, please with pink flowers and honey on . . . ' she pleaded.

'OK,' Bryn relented, swinging his legs over the side of the sofa. 'Just for a bit, Da. Then I really have to study till Mum gets in.'

Darya snuggled up to him. She sucked her thumb contentedly. On the screen, three happy and enthusiastic young presenters and a dog were demonstrating how to make useless things out of egg cartons and cereal boxes. Bryn remembered the programme from when he was little.

Bryn and Darya watched until the programme ended. Then Darya flicked the remote. 'Wow!' she breathed as the screen burst into luridly coloured life and a tinkly tune filled the room. 'Look, Bryn: *Mini-Baby Eco-Warriors*. My favourite.'

Bryn allowed the mindless cartoon to wash over him. It was like drowning in sweet, thick candy-coloured icing, he thought. Gradually, his head began to fill with pink fluff, until even his teeth started feeling gummy. Finally, his brain signalled time-out.

4

'That's enough, Da,' he said, getting up. 'I have to work.'

Darya went, 'Aww . . .', pulled a discontented face, though her eyes never left the screen. 'OK, see you,' she sighed. Relieved to be getting away so easily—Darya's sulks were legendary and could go on for days—Bryn headed for the stairs.

'Bryn . . .'

Groaning, Bryn returned, stuck his head round the door. 'What do you want now?' he said crossly. Was he never going to get time on his own?

Darya looked up at him, her eyes huge blue pools. Her lower lip quivered. 'I miss Dad,' she gulped. 'I miss him so much.'

Bryn cursed himself for his insensitivity. She was only a kid, he reminded himself. A little kid. He crossed the room, sat on the arm of the couch, gave Darya a hug. 'So do I, Da,' he said softly. 'So do I.'

Darya cuddled into him, laid her head on his shoulder. 'Do you think we'll be all right?' she asked.

'Sure.' Bryn injected a note of confident brightness into his voice. 'We've got Mum. And each other, haven't we? You bet we'll be all right. All right for ever and ever.'

Darya sighed contentedly. 'You promise you won't ever leave me?' she said.

'I'll never leave you, Da,' Bryn told her. 'I promise.'

Bryn went upstairs. He had to be so careful around Darya. She was bright, quick to catch on to things. And she got upset faster than a house of cards. A small firework, that was what their dad had called her. Light the blue touchpaper and stand well back.

Bryn stood in the doorway of his room. He listened. Nothing. Darya seemed to have settled down again in front

5

of the TV. He closed his door quietly and locked it. Just in case. He didn't want her coming in unexpectedly and seeing what he was up to. Right now, he didn't want anybody seeing anything.

From a cupboard in the wall above his bed, Bryn carefully lifted out a flat black box, about a foot square. He carried it over to his work area. He set the box gently down on the desk, raising the lid to reveal a keyboard set into a recessed area under a black screen. As soon as the lid was raised, the screen lit up. There was a low whirring noise. Bryn sat down and waited. After a few seconds, there was a loud fanfare, as if something very important was about to happen. Then the box spoke:

'Hello, Bryn.' Its voice was metallic, stilted.

'Er . . . hi, Ned.'

'Have you had a nice day?'

'Umm . . . whatever. You know.'

'I have been working on the tasks you set me.'

'That's great, Ned.'

'I have written your history essay and I have the answers to your maths homework ready.'

'Nice one.'

'I have calculated them to the nearest eight decimal places. I hope that is satisfactory.'

'Fine, Ned. That's fine.'

'Is that all—or is there anything more I can do for you?' The voice sounded a bit aggrieved as if doing Bryn's homework was slightly beneath its dignity.

'Not right now. Not unless you know how to reach level 9 in Ecotron Raiders.'

There was a few seconds' silence whilst the box thought about this. Numbers flashed in random sequences on the screen. At last the voice admitted reluctantly and a bit sulkily: 'I am sorry, I do not understand your command.'

'No stress, Ned.' Bryn grinned. 'After your time, eh?'

'Is there anything else?' the voice asked hopefully.

'Nope. Just hang around for a bit.'

The soft whirring noise grew fractionally louder for a second, as if something deep inside the black box was sighing. Then the screen went blank. Bryn pulled a face. The computer was definitely getting worse. It had never liked doing homework. Now, just to make its status and its attitude perfectly clear, it had decided to announce itself with a fanfare.

Bryn wished his dad was here. He'd know what to do with Ned. His dad had found the computer in the techno-store on the outskirts of town. He and Bryn used to go there on Saturday mornings. You could buy computer bygones and collectibles. His dad liked fixing them up. Fixing Ned was his dad's latest project. Now he'd gone, leaving the machine and its strange quirks to Bryn. Getting to grips with Ned was proving to be a steep learning curve. Bryn had never come across a computer with a voice-response mechanism. In his experience, computers were chips, memory boards, and circuits. You played games on them, did schoolwork, went on Globenet. His relationship with Ned was slightly more complex, although he kept telling himself it wasn't. After all, Ned was a machine. Machines didn't have personalities. They could not make choices, express opinions.

Bryn knew Ned was very old—maybe more than a hundred years, his dad reckoned. It dated back to the first part of the millennium. Before the Cybercrash. Theoretically, Ned should have been easy to handle. But it wasn't working out that way. Ned was unpredictable, erratic. And often plain rude. Sometimes Bryn got so cross with the computer, he felt like smashing it into a thousand pieces. But he didn't. Thanks to Ned, his grades had finally started going up.

And there was something else. Somewhere in the machine's memory he hoped there might be a clue to his dad's death. For Bryn knew, with fierce certainty, that it had not been the result of a 'freak accident at work'. That was a lie. His father didn't have accidents. Somebody had deliberately and cold-bloodedly arranged his death. Bryn was determined to find out who had killed him and why.

Beta

J ade. Jay-duh. It was a stupid name, she thought. Why on earth had they given her such a stupid name? Jade sighed. As if she didn't know, she thought. As if they hadn't told her. Time after time after time until she could repeat it like a mantra:

It is the name of a precious stone ('very rare and beautiful').

It has magical powers ('the wearer gets strength and spirituality').

It is very expensive to buy ('we spent months finding the right clinic').

Jade.

Chosen child.

Miracle of genetic engineering.

Tuesdays, Jade thought to herself. She could never quite get the hang of Tuesdays. This Tuesday followed the same pattern as the others. She woke at seven after another nightmare-ridden sleep. It was the one about the world coming to an end and the four horsemen again. This time it had been so real that when she opened her eyes, she could still hear the drumming of hooves, still see the colours of the four riders; so clear that she could hear the sounds of the battle, the high-pitched screams of the dying.

Jade had woken suddenly. For a few seconds she had lain, dislocated, in the pale primrose light of dawn. Her heart beat wildly and fear held her in its icy grip. It was always the same after waking from this one: a deep terror, a feeling that the world was ending around her and that she could do nothing to prevent it. Then she saw the familiar outlines of her bedroom. She had lain, arms folded behind her head, letting the horrors of the night fade away.

Jade left it until the very last minute before she got up and dressed. She shrugged into her clothes, the same ones she'd worn the day before. She ran her fingers a couple of times through her long black hair, which she had left loose and hanging down her back. The other girls in her class braided every tiny strand of hair, before decorating it with 'natural found objects', feathers or flowers or tiny stones with holes, but Jade had neither the time or the inclination to do her hair like everyone else. Nor was she bothered about what she wore. Any old top and trousers sufficed. Jade went downstairs. She got her own breakfast. Her parents left for work early. She would get her own tea too. Probably she'd be in bed long before they arrived home. It was lonely being chosen.

Jade arrived at the school gate. The bell had just gone. The usual crowd of girls from her class was hanging around the entrance. The razor blades in Jade's candyfloss. Only there to give grief. Jade tried to slink past unnoticed. As if.

'Hey, nice *hair*, Jade,' one girl said.

Jade stuck her chin in the air.

'Yeah, great style!' somebody else added.

Jade pretended not to hear.

'And I just *love* your clothes—where do you find them?'

'At the local recycling plant, huh?'

Jade ignored them. Like she did every day. She marched into school, head held high, refusing to react to the taunting words. She wasn't going to compromise her principles for the sake of popularity. She was an individual, she told herself. Not a fashion clone.

Looking back, Jade found it hard to remember how she had actually spent the rest of that schoolday. She must have gone to lessons and maybe, although she couldn't now recall it, she had eaten lunch in the big cafeteria. She didn't remember anybody speaking to her—though perhaps somebody had. It was as if her dream life was taking over. Step by step, she was losing contact with reality. More and more, Jade seemed to inhabit a strange twilight world, where she was forever struggling, panic-stricken, through a grey landscape, trying without success to reach some unknown destination, whilst at her back, she could hear the endless drumming of hooves, the jingling of harness, the sounds of battle. The question Jade asked herself constantly was: what was going on? Closely followed by: why me?

Then it was four o'clock, the end of the school day. Everybody started streaming out of the building. Jade went to her special corner of the park, where the river flowed past green banks and there was a small rustic bridge artistically placed so that people could lean over the side and admire the view. She crept in under the bridge and sat watching the clear water flow by on its way to somewhere. She stayed there for hours, lost in her own thoughts until she woke up, realized it was late in the afternoon and remembered the special history assignment due in tomorrow.

Panic set in. If she failed to hand in yet another piece of work, her parents would have to be summoned to the school. It was a threat that Jade took extremely seriously. She didn't want to cause any trouble with the parents who had chosen her like they'd choose any store-bought item, but who worked such long hours that they hardly ever saw her any more. She knew from past experience that her teacher Mr Neots would cream her if she didn't produce something. She got up and started walking, racking her brain to try and remember what she was supposed to study. She vaguely recalled something about the harvest failure of 2049, but she wasn't sure. Jade walked on, wondering what on earth to do. Then she recognized the name of the street she was on, realized that she was just about to pass Bryn's house. She decided to call in and see if he had the relevant notes.

Jade didn't usually speak to Bryn. He was a boy, he was popular. Two good reasons to ignore him. But he was in her history class, he had not laughed at her recently, and she was desperate enough to try anything. She went up the path and knocked loudly on the door. There was a pause. She heard the sound of running footsteps in the hall. A small girl's voice asked: 'Who is it?'

Jade said, 'Jade. I'm in Bryn's class at school. Is he there?'

'Yes,' the girl answered. There was a longer pause. Jade stood and waited to be let in. When nothing happened she said, 'Look, can you open the door, I want to have a quick word with him.'

'I'm not allowed to open the door to strangers,' came the baffling reply.

Jade thought swiftly. 'Then can you go and get him?' she asked.

'OK,' said the girl. Jade heard the sound of her footsteps pattering away.

More time passed. Then the door was opened. Bryn was there. He looked at her, a puzzled expression on his face.

'Yeah?' he queried.

Jade took a deep breath. 'Umm . . . it's about our history assignment,' she said.

Bryn went on staring at her whilst she explained. He recognized her, of course: the weird girl who sat in front of him. He had never paid her any attention. She was a bit

12

of a loner. Wore scruffy clothes. Seemed to have no friends. He'd also got the idea that she was regarded as the class fall guy by the rest of the girls. Now, staring down at her, Bryn was suddenly struck by her eyes, dark-brown with gold flecks, the colour of autumn leaves. They were fringed by thick black lashes, and set wide apart in her oval-shaped face. Her long hair streamed over her shoulders. He had never noticed how very black it was— like a raven's wing. It made her skin look almost luminous in the glow of the early evening light. Bryn realized that though he'd seen Jade nearly every day, he'd never really *looked* at her before. He had not recognized how beautiful she was.

'You'd better come in,' he said.

Jade stepped inside. 'Is it OK?' she asked.

'No problem.' Bryn led her into the living room.

Jade looked around. Amazing. Scuffed furniture, saggy couch, toys on the floor; there was even evidence of food being consumed here. People lived like this? In her parents' house, rooms were arranged to look good, not to mess up. In her parents' house, everything looked new, shiny, untouched. Surfaces gleamed. Things were not dumped on the floor. Not ever. Meals were consumed only in the tiny eating area, the debris quickly tidied away.

'Sit down.'

Gingerly, Jade lowered herself on to the messy couch. Darya immediately sat down next to her.

'Umm . . . I was wondering if I could borrow your notes—if you've finished with them,' Jade said.

'Sure. I'll go get them.'

Bryn disappeared. Jade sat awkwardly on the edge of the couch. Darya hadn't taken her eyes off her. It was disconcerting to be watched so closely. She tried giving the little girl a cautious smile.

'What's your name again?' Darya instantly asked.

'Jade.'

'My name's Darya. I'm Bryn's sister,' Darya told her. She slid an arm through Jade's arm, leaned against her. Jade moved uneasily away. She was not used to intimacy.

Bryn returned, carrying a folder. 'Here, you can borrow these.'

'Won't you need them for your assignment?' Jade asked, getting up quickly.

'No problem. I already finished mine.' Bryn held out the folder. He wasn't going to let on that Ned had spent all day writing it.

'Well . . . if you're sure,' Jade said gratefully. All she had to do now was get home, she thought, read the notes, write something vaguely coherent. 'So . . . ' she said, edging towards the door, 'umm, yeah . . . thanks again.'

Bryn was intrigued. Jade made as little eye contact as possible. It was as if she'd rather talk to the floor, the wall, anything but him. All at once, he wanted to find out more about this mysterious girl. He positioned himself in the open doorway, leaned casually against the frame. She'd have to physically push him aside to get past, he thought.

'Live far?' he asked.

'Over by the park,' Jade muttered.

Bryn's eyes widened. Rich territory. He didn't know anyone who lived there. Jade glanced at him, saw the look on his face. He doesn't believe me, she thought. He's just like the rest of them. Judging by appearances. She felt her spirits sink. This had been a big mistake.

'Hey, I'll walk you,' Bryn said.

'No, I don't want you to,' Jade replied quickly.

'Yeah, it's no trouble. Come on.' Bryn hurried Jade to the front door. He pretended not to hear Darya's plea to come too. 'See you later, Da. Cover for me with Mum,' he called over his shoulder, closing the door behind them.

The light was beginning to fade gently. Jade walked as fast as she could. She wanted to get home, rid herself of Bryn. She felt a growing irritation. She only wanted to borrow some notes. It was not an invitation to invade her space. Anyway, he didn't like her. He kept staring at her. He was only doing this so he could check her out, report back to his mates. Tomorrow, they'd all have a good laugh at her expense.

Bryn kept pace with her. He'd never walked a girl like Jade home before. In his experience, girls flirted, laughed, clung on to his arm and looked up at him. Tried to make the walk last as long as possible. This girl hurried along slightly in front of him, her face set and expressionless. She did not say anything. Even when they reached the high wall and electronic gate that separated the huge houses where the rich people lived apart from the rest of the world.

Jade walked up to the gate, held her wrist in front of it. A beam scanned an invisible something. The gate glided noiselessly open. Jade almost ran through. The gate silently closed. Bryn shrugged. Be like that then, he thought. No problem. He listened to her footsteps walking away into the twilight.

Jade opened the door to her house. Silence. Emptiness. Wearily, she leaned her head against the cool white wall. Well done, she told herself. You really screwed up. The most popular, best looking boy in the class walks you home and you don't say a single word. Stupid, stupid! Jade banged her head against the wall a couple of times. Why did she always think the worst of people? Why was she so defensive all the time? What was wrong with her?

And then, unbidden and unwelcome, she heard them. Distant at first, like the approach of thunder. The horses were coming. They rapidly got closer and clearer until she seemed surrounded by invisible figures galloping in the darkness. Jade's eyes stared in front of her, misty, unfixed. She began rocking backwards and forwards. Words rose up into her mind. Strange, terrifying. Alone in the empty house, Jade chanted softly:

> *I hear the riders in the night,*
> *The four horsemen are coming soon.*
> *I hear the sound of their harness jingle*
> *Drumming of hooves on the open road.*
> *The first horse is white and a king rides upon it.*
> *The second is red, the colour of blood.*
> *The third is black and famine follows it.*
> *The fourth horse is pale and its rider is Death.*

Outside the gate, Bryn waited. Perhaps she'd change her mind, he thought hopefully. Perhaps she'd come back. He peered through the bars. He couldn't believe Jade really lived here. He'd never seen anything like this place. The houses were vast, set back from the road. There were so many trees. He wondered what the area was called. He looked all round but couldn't find a name. That said it all. This place was so posh it didn't need a name. Just a high wall, a security system, and an electronic gate to keep everybody else out.

While he waited, Bryn thought about place names. It seemed that the more run down the neighbourhood, the nicer its name. Probably why the area by the motorway and the sewage works was called Paradise Park, he thought. Because it wasn't a park. There wasn't even a blade of grass. Bryn and his mates didn't go there. Nobody he knew went there. Not unarmed. The kids from Paradise Park were known as Slab-rats. After the flat grey high-rises they lived in. Nobody messed with them. Bryn waited a bit longer. Jade didn't come. He went home.

Gamma

Mr Neots, teacher—or educator, as he preferred to call himself—was a deeply unhappy man. He hated his job. He hated the school and, most of all, he hated the students. Or as he preferred to call them: the miserable specimens of adolescent prurience.

This class was his least favourite. Not that he had any favourite classes. Or favourite anything. His despite was pretty universal.

'Life in the early part of the twenty-first century . . . ' Mr Neots snarled, glaring quickly round the room to check everybody was busy getting down his words.

Bryn bent his head obediently over his work station. He didn't want to admit that he was frightened of Mr Neots but there was something scary about the guy. He felt it, they all did. The hatred was totally mutual.

'At that time,' Mr Neots continued, 'the world was a very different place. There were more continents . . . ' He paused, glanced down at a girl in the front row. 'That's c...o...n...t...i...n...e...n...t...s, Jena—a land mass of considerable size. The names of some of these continents were: Europe, Africa, Australia, and a vast land mass called the United States.'

'What happened to them, sir?' Gil asked.

'I am about to tell you,' Mr Neots snapped, 'that is, if you will do me the kindness NOT to interrupt.' He froze Gil with an icy glare.

'Sorry, sir.' Gil flushed, looked down at his work.

'In the years leading up to 2040, the earth suffered a

series of natural disasters. These included floods, cyclones, and tidal waves. Many land masses were reduced in size or disappeared altogether. Large areas of the world became depopulated by a virus called HIV.' Mr Neots checked Jena's work again, tutted and rolled his eyes upwards. 'The emissions of what were called "greenhouse gases" resulted in the planet becoming much hotter,' he went on, 'so that in 2047, volcanic eruptions in several continents were followed by extreme climate change, resulting in the three years of global harvest failure from 2049 to 2051. As a result, over a third of the remaining world's population died from disease or starvation.'

Mr Neots began prowling along the rows of desks. He stopped in front of one, held out his hand. The student meekly handed him a small bag of sweets. Mr Neots pocketed the bag, gave the student an evil look, resumed walking.

'I look forward to reading your assessment of this time—I trust you have them?' His tone was light, almost careless, but nobody failed to pick up the underlying menace.

Bryn felt in his bag. The work was there. Nice one, Ned, he thought. It was great having a homework machine. All he'd had to do was let it scan his class notes, type in the assignment title, tell it how many pages he wanted, and in a couple of hours, Ned produced the essay. Bryn hadn't bothered to check it, but he was sure it was OK. He wondered if Jade had finished her assignment. Bryn looked up. Jade sat hunched in a shaft of sunlight which touched her hair with dark fire. She was staring fixedly out of the window, her hands idle upon her keyboard. Bryn noticed the bird-brittle neck bones at the base of her skull where the hair parted. So delicate. Amazing. He'd never seen anything so beautiful. Forgetting the task in hand, he focused upon the back of Jade's head.

'At this time,' Mr Neots continued remorselessly, 'the population of the world was fragmented into countries and tribes . . . ' He checked Jena's spelling again, nodded and passed on. 'Wars broke out frequently. There were over 193 autonomous polities. It was a barbaric and uncivilized time. A recipe for disaster.' He paused. 'Unlike now . . . ' he said.

Bryn sighed, dragged his mind away from Jade. Here we go again, he thought. The big lecture. He looked round. Everybody wore the kind of fascinated expression which meant they weren't listening.

'Now, we have peace. We have order. Thanks to our single, centralized planetary authority, our world no longer suffers from unpredictable climate, or unprovoked conflict.' Mr Neots's face took on an enraptured expression. Bored glances were exchanged. They'd heard it all before. Practically every lesson.

'Our global government ensures that everybody on the planet has everything they need to survive well into the twenty-third century . . . our President—'

A buzzer sounded in the corridor. Everyone started to pack up.

'Assignments on my desk!' Mr Neots snapped.

Bryn pulled out his essay. Gil leaned across the aisle.

'Geez, he gets worse, doesn't he?' he remarked.

'Err . . . yeah,' Bryn muttered. He looked around. Jade had vanished.

Bryn and Gil stood by the vending machine. The vending machine was close to the girls' cloakroom. Bryn hoped Jade was in the cloakroom. It was where girls always went between classes. Bryn couldn't begin to imagine what they did in there, but they always emerged giggling and laughing. Girls. An unknown species. A different tribe. A recipe for disaster. He liked them, but he didn't understand them at all. Idly, Bryn ran his finger over the blue and silver Globemart logo on the side of the machine.

'What is that guy like?' Gil was still indignant. He never got into trouble. He was serious about his studies, hoped to get into college one day. Bryn nodded, only half-listening, his eyes were fixed on the cloakroom door.

'And why does he go on about politics all the time,' Gil said angrily. 'I mean, who gives a toss?'

'Right.'

It was true, Bryn thought. Neots was always lecturing them about how bad things used to be compared with now. As if anyone was bothered. Who cared about the past? So long as they could listen to their music, go out, buy clothes, life was sweet. A party. And he was always going on about how wonderful the President was. Boring. As if anyone was interested in who ruled the world. For all they cared, the President could be a long-haired hamster.

At last the cloakroom door opened. A group of girls emerged, giggling and calling insults to whoever was still inside. Jade wasn't with them.

'Hey, Bryn.' Jena sauntered over. 'Wanta hang out after school?'

'Not sure,' Bryn said. 'Might have things to do.'

'Yeah? Maybe we could do them together, whatd'yasay?' Jena murmured. She smiled, head on one side, leaning in towards him, her mates going 'Ooohh' in the background. Bryn felt himself blushing.

'I'll see, OK.'

'Old Notty gave you a hard time, didn't he?' Gil said.

Jena tossed her blonde feather-ornamented hair, spat her gum neatly into the trashbin. She strutted a few steps and swore loudly, curling her lip. 'He's gonna get *his* one day, believe me. Old **!**.'

'Umm . . . is Jade in there?' Bryn interrupted, nodding towards the cloakroom.

'Who?'

'Jade. Sits in front of me.'

'Whatd'ya want her for?'

'Nothing. She borrowed some notes off me.'

'Yeah?' Jena's lip curled again. 'Well, betcha won't get 'em back.' She circled her index finger in front of her head. 'She's crazy. In't she?' Jena turned to her group of mates for corroboration. They nodded in agreement, giggling. 'She's a mad garbo-head,' Jena went on. She grabbed Bryn's arm. 'Forget about her, man. Concentrate on me.'

'Maybe,' Bryn replied vaguely. He and Jena had dated a while back. It had been an unforgettable experience. Though he was trying to. He really didn't want to go down that road again.

Then the cloakroom door opened. Jade came out. Jena looked over her shoulder, saw her. 'Hey, slapface,' she shouted, 'somebody wantsta speak t'ya.' Jade turned round, her face expressionless. She gave Bryn and Jena a quick glance, turned and walked away. 'See what I mean?' Jena circled her head again. 'Totally lurdo. Hospital food, that one. Wastin' ya time there.' She rejoined her mates. Laughing and chatting, they sauntered off in the opposite direction.

Gil picked up his bag. 'Coming to science?' he asked.

'In a bit. You go on.'

Gil looked at him quizzically. Bryn shrugged. Gil sighed resignedly. He shouldered his bag, set off after the gang of girls.

Meanwhile Bryn hurried after Jade. She was walking fast.

'Jade, wait up.'

Jade slowed slightly. Bryn came alongside.

'So, how are you doing?' he asked. 'Did you finish the work?'

Jade slowed some more. Then she stopped. 'Oh yeah. I forgot, sorry.' She slid her backpack off her shoulder. Took out Bryn's notes and handed them to him. 'Here, thanks for lending me your stuff.'

'No problem.' Bryn took the notes. They were damp and slightly crumpled.

'You going somewhere?' he asked.

'Why?' Jade was instantly on her guard.

'Just asking. Only we've got science now, haven't we?'

'Yeah. So?'

'So science is in that direction.' Bryn jerked his thumb over his shoulder.

'Mmm.' Jade nodded in agreement, but didn't move.

'Well?' Bryn waited. Geez, she was weird, he thought. But beautiful. You could burn up in those bonfire eyes.

'I hate that man!' Jade declared suddenly. 'He's evil!'

'Sorry?'

'Him. That man. Neots. He's evil.'

Bryn was lost. 'Oh. Er . . . I wouldn't go that far,' he stammered.

Jade's eyes were remote and watchful in her pale colourless face. 'Wouldn't you?' she muttered darkly. 'Maybe that's because you don't feel it like I do.' She glanced over her shoulder. 'Well, thanks anyway,' she said and strolled off.

Bryn thought, you can't just walk out. But Jade strode towards the exit, pushed the door open. She walked out and disappeared. Disbelieving, Bryn stared after her. She'd be in real trouble when her absence was spotted. And it would be. The school was hot on missing class. He wondered if he ought to follow and fetch her back. Bryn shot a glance at his watch: 11.30: science was about to begin. If he went after Jade, he'd be late. Then he'd be the one in trouble. He shrugged. Let her sort out her own life. He ran back along the corridor.

Jade felt she had to get out. The walls were closing in on her. She couldn't breathe properly. She had to see the sky, suck in real air. She walked swiftly across the grass towards the perimeter fence. Her heart was beating hard. Why? she asked herself. Why? She gripped her hands into tight fists. Beyond the fence, life was going on. MPVs passed carrying people on their way to work or to the Mall.

Why was she the only one to feel like this, she thought. First there was that man—the utter contempt on his face as he accepted her work. Like it was total crap. Then Bryn, ignoring her, standing so close to Jena. The hurt going in, clean as a razor. Dark blood welling. Jade stared bleakly through the fence for a bit, but there was no escape. The fence was too high to climb, the exit had a security system. She turned, walked slowly back towards the high, white, hated building. Her daily prison. She looked up. And he was there. The evil man. Standing at an upper window. Jade shuddered. She was dead meat.

Mr Neots sorted the unmarked assignments into three piles: Good, Average, and Waste of Time. He put Jade and Jena's work straight on to the last pile. He didn't even bother to open the folders. Gil's work went on the Good pile along with two other students. All the rest were consigned to the Average group. Mr Neots looked at the big pile of Average assignments. He sighed. They were so stupid, these kids. So uninteresting to teach. So mediocre. He picked up the top folder, opened it and read the opening paragraph. Then read some more. As his eye travelled down the page, the next page and the next, a curious expression came over his thin, unpleasant face. A mixture of amazement and disbelief. He turned the folder over, read the name on the front, checked his marklist.

Mr Neots replaced the folder, sat down at his desk. The boy was trying to have a joke at his expense. Yes. That was the explanation. He must have made it up. He re-read the first page, frowned. It didn't read like a joke though. Not at all. But how had he obtained this information? Mr Neots got up, wandered over to the window, the assignment in his hand. The boy had never learned this in his class. He only taught the prescribed global curriculum. To the syllable. Nothing more, nothing less. Somehow, this boy must have got access to some secondary sources. Illegal ones. Mr Neots stared out unseeingly across the school grounds. If his government contact heard about this, he thought, he would be in trouble. Serious trouble. It was his job to make sure the students learned only what the government said. He was definitely not supposed to tolerate free thought, nor encourage alternative interpretations of the facts.

Should this boy's work be read by others, Mr Neots thought to himself, he could kiss goodbye to his chances of ever leaving teaching. For a brief and terrible moment, Mr Neots contemplated a future stuck inside the classroom. He saw in his imagination an endless sea of blank, uninterested faces. He shuddered. He was not going to let it happen. Oh no. He was going to have to take steps. And it was not going to be pleasant for the student concerned, Mr Neots decided grimly. Not pleasant at all.

Delta

Next evening, Bryn found the envelope. He had gone to the shed to get one of the tiny screwdrivers. He knew his father kept them in a drawer under the workbench. The envelope was taped to the bottom of the drawer. Bryn peeled the envelope off, opened it up. A sheet of blank paper, neatly folded. Inside the paper, a small oblong card, made out of plastic-like material. White, with a couple of raised gold dots at one end. For a few seconds, Bryn stared at the card, trying to work out what it was for, why it was hidden away. Then he slipped it into his pocket and went back to the house. The card could wait. He had more important things to deal with right now.

Ned had been particularly annoying lately. Bryn had discovered the strange computer could adopt several personalities. He'd found them whilst fiddling with the keypad. There was the Ned who was good at doing homework, useless at anything else. Then there was a lady Ned. She was naggy and bad tempered. As if she had permanent PMT. However both Neds paled into insignificance compared with the third incarnation: Ned the toddler. Two minutes of Ned's inner child had Bryn reaching for a hammer! The trouble was that now Ned kept changing personalities all the time. Bryn decided he must have loosened something inside when he got so stressed with little Ned that he'd picked the machine up and shaken it. He refused to believe that the machine was doing it deliberately. That was why he'd gone looking for the screwdriver. He had to fix Ned before it drove him crazy.

Bryn picked up the computer, turned it over looking for things to unbolt.

'Are you sure you should be doing that?' Ned asked anxiously.

'Yeah, it's OK,' Bryn said reassuringly.

'Geddoff, nasty boy,' little Ned whined.

'Shut it!' Bryn growled.

The computer made 'I'm-not-happy-about-this' noises as Bryn tipped it one way then another searching for something to undo. There was nothing. The machine seemed to have been made in one fluid piece. Bryn swore under his breath.

'Umm . . . that was a rude word!' little Ned said self-righteously.

Bryn put the machine down again. There must be some way into it, he thought. He slid his fingers slowly along the edges of the keyboard, searching for something, anything that might give him access. He found the slot. Bryn tipped Ned up, tried to insert the screwdriver into the narrow aperture. It didn't work. He felt a wave of frustration. If only his dad were here. He pictured his dad working on other computers. It didn't help, but it reminded him of the white card he'd found earlier. Bryn pulled the card out of his pocket. He needed a temporary distraction. He looked at it, looked at Ned, and something clicked in his brain. A connection.

Bryn pushed the card into the side slot. Ned made a low whirring sound. The card slid into the machine and disappeared. Bryn lowered the computer onto the desk. He sat down in front of the screen and waited to see what would happen next.

The same evening, in a different part of town, Mr Neots was studying the members of his family, assembled round the supper table, and asking himself yet again why he bothered with any of them.

He watched his wife, a colourless woman, morosely forking up food. What a waste of space, he thought. A dull, lifeless drab. He despised her.

His cold, stern gaze continued to sweep round the table.

Kirrin, his thirteen-year-old son, felt a shiver run through him. He dreaded mealtimes. Long, unfilled silences, broken only by bitter exchanges between his parents or, even worse, having to find answers to questions fired at him about his day. He kept his head down, concentrated upon shovelling food quickly into his mouth. Maybe there would be a pudding today, he thought. Perhaps he might get seconds if he ate quickly.

Mr Neots regarded Kirrin scornfully. What a mooncalf. Only interested in filling his stomach. No brain, no initiative. Nothing like himself when he was young. He frowned angrily at his son. Kirrin tried to pretend he hadn't seen him.

'What's for dessert?' eight-year-old Kallie piped up from the far end of the table. At the sound of her shrill voice, Mr Neots's stern face relaxed. The ghost of a smile crept across his face. Kallie, with her red curls and her bossy, imperious demands, was his only weakness. Kallie was the sole member of the family who could always get her way with him.

Mrs Neots rose clumsily from her chair and went into the kitchen to fetch the pudding and the set of bowls. In silence, she dished out bright orange mousse and, in silence, the family consumed it. The only sound came from Kallie who made disgusting sucking noises with her spoon. Kirrin knew she was doing it on purpose to get attention. Neither of his parents reprimanded her. As soon as he had finished, Mr Neots got up and pushed back his chair.

'I'm going out,' he announced. 'I don't know when I shall be back.'

His wife looked at him warily but made no comment.

'Are you going to see the man with the posh grey car?' Kallie asked. 'Can I come with you, Daddy?'

Mr Neots glanced down affectionately at her eager little face. 'Not tonight,' he said, patting her head. 'You stay here and do your homework and I just *might* have something special to tell you when I get back.'

'Goody!' Kallie bounced up and down on her chair. 'A secret?'

Mr Neots nodded. 'A secret,' he repeated. He strode out of the room. Kallie ran after him. Kirrin heard them going down the hallway, then the front door slamming. He glanced across at his mother, sitting white-faced in her place, her pudding untouched in her bowl.

Without being asked, Kirrin started collecting the crockery, piling it up neatly. When he had cleared the table, he transferred everything to the kitchen. Coming back into the room, he saw that his mother had poured herself a large drink.

'OK, Mum?' Kirrin asked. She nodded.

Kirrin made his way upstairs to his room, shut the door. Let them get on with it, he thought. He sat down in front of his computer, selected a game. The screen filled with scaly, two-headed, black spacelizards. Picking up the remote controlled laser-gun, Kirrin aimed and fired. Again and again he shot at the screen, working himself into a frenzy of killing as one by one the repulsive alien reptiles collapsed and died in terrible torment. If only . . . his brain kept repeating, if only . . .

For a nanosecond, Ned's screen remained blank. Then, an image began to evolve, growing out of the fuzzy

28

background like a ghost. It got clearer, bigger, closer. Bryn gasped, felt his heart pounding. It was a hologram of his father. He was wearing his weekend clothes—the same ones Bryn remembered him wearing just before he died.

'Hello, Bryn,' his father said. 'I knew you'd find the calling card sooner or later. Sorry that I'm no longer there with you. I wonder what they told you. Accident at work? Yes, probably an accident. That would be the most convenient, wouldn't it. Nobody's fault. Just one of those unfortunate things.' He smiled, but there was sadness around his eyes. Bryn caught his breath. He so desperately wanted to put out his hand, touch his father's face one more time. The pain was almost unbearable.

'I've decided to make this hologram to leave you a little something to remember me by,' his father went on.

Bryn gulped. He recollected seeing an incident like this recently on an old movie. He remembered sneering— it had seemed so corny and clichéd. Now, he wasn't laughing. He stared at the hologram, trying to read the thoughts behind his dad's eyes. But there was nothing in his father's expression or measured tone of voice to suggest anything other than complete normality.

'I just wanted to tell you how much I love you, son,' his dad said, 'and how proud I am of the way you're growing up.'

Bryn blinked, wiped his eyes with the back of his sleeve.

'Oh, and I need to tell you a few facts about Ned . . . '

Don't bother, Bryn told him silently. Ned's a total waste of space and effort. You don't have to tell me. I already know.

'Ned's extremely special,' his father went on. 'It's not like a normal machine. I think Ned's a prototype, a one off. I'm guessing there's no other computer like it on the planet. It has all sorts of strange programmes—I expect you've found some of them already, knowing you! There are a lot of amazing things in there. Even I haven't been able to get at everything that's stored in its memory. But I do know that Ned's got the power to do things a Globecomp machine can't do. It can change things, alter them. Maybe for good, maybe not. I haven't had time to work that one out. So you have to be very careful, Bryn. Don't tell anybody. If word gets out that Ned exists, well . . . it wouldn't be a good idea.' He paused, grimaced. 'I can't say any more, sorry. Just be careful, son, that's all. Promise me. And look after Mum and Darya, won't you. I know I can rely on you to do that.'

The image faded. Bryn stared hungrily at the screen, willing his father to come back.

There was silence. Then things whirred and hummed deep inside the machine. 'The information on this card has been processed,' Ned said. 'Unfortunately it is not compatible with any existing files. I am therefore unable to retain and store it.' The computer sounded pleased with itself, as if it had imparted something really important.

'Never mind that, just get my father back again, will you,' Bryn commanded.

'I am sorry, this information is not on file,' Ned told him.

'Find it!' Bryn raised his voice.

'Regrettably I am unable to comply with your request,' Ned repeated tonelessly. 'As it is incompatible with my filing systems, all information on the card has been deleted.'

The white card slid smoothly out of the slot.

Bryn pushed the card back inside. 'I didn't tell you to do that!' he shouted. 'You can't make decisions on your own. You have to find my dad again.'

'I am sorry, I cannot comply with your request,' Ned said flatly. 'Have a nice day.'

30

The card reappeared.

'No!' Bryn shouted. He repeated the process. Again. And again. Each time, Ned returned the card. Finally, Bryn understood. His father had gone. He would never see him again. He laid his head on the desk and let the tears come.

Mr Neots returned late that evening, sober and thoughtful. Kirrin heard his key in the lock, his footsteps on the stairs. He opened a book and pretended to be studying.

Without knocking, Mr Neots came into Kirrin's room. His face bore its usual unpleasant, sarcastic expression but Kirrin sensed an underlying air of suppressed excitement. Mr Neots strode over to the desk and picked up one of Kirrin's books, flipped the pages. Kirrin waited, prepared himself.

'Still at work?'

Kirrin nodded. Something was up. Mr Neots picked up Kirrin's green pen, his favourite. He unscrewed the top. Kirrin watched him apprehensively. It wouldn't be the first time his father had destroyed one of his treasured possessions in a fit of anger.

'So, Kirrin,' Mr Neots spoke casually, 'do you know a boy called Bryn?'

Kirrin nodded. Everybody knew Bryn. He was good looking, a computer game genius, popular with girls. Bryn was everything that Kirrin longed to be himself.

'I would like you to become friends with Bryn,' Mr Neots said replacing the pen.

Kirrin gasped in astonishment. 'But,' he stammered, 'he's older than me.'

'So what?' his father snapped. 'You both like computer games, don't you? That's a good start to a friendship.'

'But . . . ' Kirrin protested feebly, 'he's very popular. I don't know how I'd even get him to talk to me.'

31

Mr Neots took hold of Kirrin's top and pulled him slowly to his feet until Kirrin's face was a couple of centimetres from his own. 'Maybe that's something that you're just going to have to work on, aren't you?' he said softly.

Kirrin swallowed. The pressure around his neck was making him feel dizzy. 'OK,' he gasped, 'I'll give it a try.' Mr Neots released his hold. Kirrin sank thankfully into his seat. He sighed. He knew that he had to obey his father. He was too scared of the consequences if he refused. He hated him, but he feared him. Fear was a great personal motivator.

'I'll try to see him tomorrow,' he promised.

In the darkened hallway outside Kirrin's room, Kallie sat motionless. She hugged her knees with her hands. Kallie's ear was pressed against Kirrin's door. She listened carefully, smiling to herself. Kirrin was useless, she thought. Totally useless. He couldn't befriend a paper bag. Besides, who'd want to be his friend? Stupid fat pig! Kallie wrinkled her small pointy nose in disgust.

Bryn must be doing something bad. Very bad. Daddy wanted to find out. Kallie's mouth curved in a secret smile. She would help Daddy. She would find out the secret. But how? Her eyes narrowed for a few minutes as she thought hard. Then she remembered: Darya. She had forgotten all about Darya. Darya was Bryn's sister; she was bound to know all about him. Kallie nodded wisely to herself. She would befriend Darya and get herself invited over to Darya's house for tea. Then she would worm the secret out of her. She had ways of doing this. Kallie got silently to her feet and tiptoed along the landing back to her own room.

Epsilon

Later that same evening in a big silent house on an estate with no name, Jade lay on her bed, contemplating her life. It was not good. Things were downward spiralling at alarming speed. She couldn't go on like this, she thought. It was making her too miserable. She had to effect some changes. She had to regain some control. Jade thought hard. She decided that some things—the weird dreams, the sense of impending doom, the vibes she got off certain people, the things she could see that nobody else saw—all these were beyond her ability to alter.

But there were other areas. A change of image might be a possibility. With this in mind, Jade spent time sewing up the holes in her clothes, trying different ways with her hair. While there was room for improvement, there was room for hope. She knew she'd never be popular or a boy magnet, but maybe if she tried a bit harder, some people might notice her. No. Jade corrected herself. She hated admitting the truth but it had to be faced: maybe *Bryn* might notice her.

As if.

Next morning Jade arrived at the school gate to be greeted with the same stupid comments as always. She shrugged it off. She wasn't discouraged. Today the shark park's opinion didn't count. She hung around the entrance hall, waiting for Bryn. He walked straight past without noticing her. Jade felt angry and disappointed with herself. She'd tried, she'd failed. It was clearly going to take more than a halfhearted make-over to change anyone's perception of her. More importantly, she'd wasted her time and compromised her principles. For what? For nothing.

Jade went straight to the girls' toilets, tore the ribbons and feathers out of her hair. She ripped a couple of holes in her sleeve and kicked her schoolbag around. Two younger girls watched in horrified amazement as Jade stamped on her hair ornaments, swearing loudly.

'Don't grow up,' Jade snarled at them. 'It doesn't get any better!'

Kallie and Darya backed hastily out of the toilets. 'What a weird girl,' Kallie said primly, smoothing her long red curls.

'She came round the other night to see my brother about something,' Darya whispered, stealing a furtive backward glance at the toilet door. She could still hear Jade kicking things.

'Well,' Kallie said, slipping her arm through Darya's, smiling very sweetly at her, 'I'm glad she's not *my* new bestest friend.'

Jade finished raging round the toilets and emerged, scruffy and unkempt, a bad case of post-traumatic dress disorder. She felt as attractive as roadkill. She stumbled down the corridor to her first class. On the way, she passed Bryn and Gil going in the opposite direction. Neither boy noticed her. Jade wished she was dead.

At lunchtime, Bryn and Gil went over to the computer centre. It was full of students playing games, catching up on study projects, sending each other messages. 'I'm going to check my mail,' Bryn told Gil. He gave the machine his password.

'Bet you've got the usual stuff,' Gil grinned. Bryn pulled

a face at him. The screen filled with **'Hi, Bryn, luv U'** written in huge pink letters. Bryn groaned. A group of younger girls over the far side of the room burst into loud screams of laughter.

'Great to be popular, eh?' Gil teased.

'Leave it out,' Bryn grunted. He checked the message box again. It was empty. What did he expect? More messages from his dad? There was nothing. There would be nothing. Bryn stared at the blank screen. He was finding it hard to centre his thoughts.

Next to him, Gil worked industriously on his homework. 'If I get this done, I can come round to yours after school,' he remarked. 'That's if we survive Old Neots,' Gil went on. His normally placid face flushed. 'I tell you, mate, if he tries it on this afternoon—well—he'd just better *not*, that's all.'

Bryn smiled, in spite of himself. Gil was into violence like girls were into three-dimensional chess. 'Yeah, sure, mate,' he said. 'You'll show him.'

Kirrin came into the computer centre. He looked around, saw Bryn and Gil. He started edging cautiously towards them. What on earth was he going to say? he thought. Of all the things his father had made him do, this was the most impossible. Just as he reached them, Bryn and Gil got up, picked up their bags. Kirrin was seized with desperation. Bryn was going. He hadn't spoken to him. His father would be cross, he'd be punished. Unsure what to do, he stood in the middle of the room, gloom settling upon him like a raincloud. Then, fate offered Kirrin a lifeline. As they passed by, deep in conversation, Bryn's bag bumped his shoulder.

'Sorry,' Bryn said, glancing at Kirrin briefly.

'It's OK,' Kirrin replied.

Well, he told himself, he'd made contact. It was a start.

Jade's head was buzzing. She'd eaten nothing since last night. Too selfconscious to enter the canteen at lunchtime, she'd lurked by the perimeter fence watching traffic. Now, she sat in class, staring straight ahead, hoping no one would notice her. She was finding it impossible to concentrate. There was a dull roaring sound in her ears and her eyes smarted painfully.

Behind her, Bryn was barely paying Mr Neots any attention either. He felt as if he were running through a maze. There was no pattern, no centre. Just alleyways leading to alleyways leading to nowhere.

Meanwhile, at the front of the classroom, Mr Neots droned on. 'You will be pleased to hear that I have marked your homework,' he said, picking up the pile of assignments on his desk. 'Some of them were promising.' He didn't hand them out, of course. Not yet. 'However, others were . . . how shall I put it? Much less promising.' He liked to make the students suffer. Make them sweat. 'The writers of those assignments will be repeating the work. After school tomorrow.' He glared round the room, including them all in his basilisk gaze. 'And I shall be contacting the parents or guardians of certain individuals to discuss their future.' He paused, waited, knowing he had their attention completely. 'If they have a future in this class that is,' he said softly. Nobody missed the menace in his voice. Even Gil felt a shiver run down his spine. The man was a sadist, he thought. He was enjoying inflicting pain.

Mr Neots began to distribute the work. Students sat cowed and silent in their seats, waiting for his fury to erupt. They did not have to wait long.

'Now this,' Mr Neots announced, holding up a dog-eared, grubby folder, 'is appalling. Truly appalling.' Everybody's eyes swivelled round to look at Jade, who was staring vacantly into space, unaware of the storm about to break over her head. Gleeful glances were exchanged. The sacrificial victim had been selected. There was a palpable air of relief mixed with happy anticipation.

Mr Neots strode quickly across the classroom. He towered over Jade. White-faced, she stared up at him. The mere effort of raising her head made crimson and orange circles form behind her eyes. The sense of evil emanating from him, which only she seemed to perceive, overpowered her. Jade began to sway backwards and forwards in her seat.

'In all my years as a teacher, I have never, ever encountered work of such truly abysmal shoddiness.' Mr Neots was winding himself up. The class relaxed. Once he had chosen his victim, the rest were guaranteed safe from a tongue lashing. In the front row Jena, the other recipient of his wrath, openly got out her pocket mirror and started fiddling with her hair, knowing she was OK for the time being.

'I have learned not to expect much from some of you, but this! This!' Mr Neots held up Jade's folder in such a way that everybody could see she'd written practically nothing. 'What kind of an idiot are you, girl? Eh, eh— answer me!' Mr Neots bent down towards Jade until his face was only centimetres from hers. Jade's gaze was wide, unfocused. Her mouth opened in mute appeal. Then, without warning, her eyes suddenly rolled upwards and she toppled sideways onto the floor at his feet.

There was a shocked silence. Mr Neots leaped back. Jade lay on her side, eyes closed, her mouth slightly open. A tiny rivulet of spit dribbled out of one corner. Mr Neots stared down at her in repelled horror. 'Get her out!' he screamed. He looked wildly around. Nobody moved. He clicked his fingers at Bryn, who sat frozen into shocked immobility. 'You, boy,' he ordered, 'get her out of here, now!'

Bryn sipped his cool drink. On the far side of the kitchen, Jade nervously nibbled a biscuit.

'You didn't have to see me home,' she said, frowning. 'I was OK as soon as I'd got out of that room.'

'No problem.' Bryn put the crystal tumbler down carefully on the white marble worktop. Any excuse to get out of Neots's class, he thought. And catch a glimpse of how the seriously rich and peculiar lived.

'I meant to do more work on the assignment.' Jade bit her lip. 'Only I ran out of time.'

'Hey, don't let Neots get to you,' Bryn said, 'he's a drekbrain. Ignore him.'

'OK for you,' Jade muttered. 'Your work wasn't bagged out.'

'Maybe he's saving me for later,' Bryn joked. He reached forward, took another sip of his drink. Ice clinked against the side of the glass. Bryn checked he hadn't slopped anything on to the white tiled floor. Everything was white in Jade's house. White walls, curtains, carpets, white leather furniture with gold legs. Even the pictures were predominantly white. Winter landscapes. Cold, clinical. Bryn wondered how Jade lived with it. She was like a snow queen, he thought. Living in a palace of ice.

'He'll contact my parents.' Jade pulled a face.

'You'll sort it.'

'They'll go postal,' Jade said gloomily. 'You don't know what they're like.'

They sat in silence for a bit. Then Jade looked at Bryn thoughtfully, as if remembering something. 'Your dad died, didn't he?' she stated calmly. 'In that explosion at the Globechem lab a couple of weeks ago. I saw it on the local news.'

Bryn nodded. He didn't know what to say.

'I don't know my real father,' Jade went on, 'my parents selected somebody from one of those . . . uh, baby-making places. You know. You give an egg, choose a father, they make the baby. They said it was a choice between a research graduate from some top university and a famous athlete and the graduate won in the end because he had dark eyes. My mum had this romantic thing about men with dark eyes.' Jade hesitated. 'Sometimes, they look at me like they wished they'd chosen the other guy.' She stopped abruptly, realizing she was sounding sorry for herself, added defiantly, 'I don't care what they think.'

'Yeah, why should you,' Bryn agreed. She's definitely weird, he thought. Weird, but beautiful and rich. It was an irresistible combination. He continued sipping his drink, wondering how he could prolong his visit. He really wanted to get to know her a bit more.

Why had she just told him all that personal stuff about her parents? Jade thought. She hardly knew him. Now he'd really think she was strange. Just like everyone else did. Jade despaired of herself. Sometimes she was sure her brain and her mouth worked independently. Especially when she felt nervous or wanted to make a good impression. Like now.

'So . . . ' Bryn finished his drink. 'You're sure you're OK?'

See what you did—he doesn't want to be here, Jade thought gloomily. He wants to go. Still, what else did she expect? Jena or some other pretty girl with nice hair ornaments and unripped clothes was probably waiting for him back at school. 'Yeah, I'm fine,' she said abruptly. She tried to keep the disappointment out of her voice.

She doesn't want me to stay, Bryn thought. Pity. Still, she probably wants to be on her own. To do whatever girls did in the privacy of their own lives. 'Well, I'll see you tomorrow then,' he said, sliding off the stool.

Jade sighed. Give up, she thought. It never worked, her and other people. Relationships were a country with unfathomable rules and elusive customs. She'd never got the hang of them. She probably never would. She led Bryn to the front door. 'You'll need my code for the main gates: it's triple six.'

Bryn nodded. 'I guess I can remember that.'

Jade shut the door. Then she ran upstairs to the front bedroom and watched Bryn walking away. She remained at the window until he disappeared from sight. After that, she went into the spotless white living room and threw all the perfectly arranged white silk cushions onto the beautifully polished whitewood floor.

It was still early. A warm, soft-aired, promise-filled summer afternoon. Too good to return to school. So Bryn decided to take the long slow route home. He turned right instead of left. Walked through neat, ungated estates. Past the huge Globemart shopping mall, where he stopped for a drink but resisted the games arcade. On to the industrial estate. To the big chemical complex where his father had worked. Jade's remark had hungered him to see it again, to relive the past one more time.

Now, when it was too late, Bryn wished he'd paid more attention to what his dad actually did. He knew it was something to do with inventing new kinds of non-fossil based fuels. He'd never really been interested. It was just a job. Until the day his dad had died. Bryn remembered that day: it had rained. The men arrived in the evening, sombre, dark-suited, rain dripping off their clothes. He had listened to their voices, quiet and respectful, hadn't believed them at first. But he saw the colour drain from his mother's face, her hands going up to her mouth, tears starting to fall. So he'd known it was true. Then something had torn inside him. He had run out of the house, pain ripping him up. He had gone down to the end of the garden and lain on the ground. That was all he could recollect. The pain, earth under his hands, and the smell of damp grass.

Now Bryn stood on the opposite side of the road. Globechem was a huge complex with massive steel and glass buildings each topped by three sky-reaching chimneys. There was a high barbed wire security fence round the outside. Bryn watched the employees coming and going. Passing through the checkpoint in an endless stream. A shift must have ended, he thought. Another shift was beginning. The same pattern repeated day in, day out. His dad had been working back the night he died. Catching up on things, he'd said. Nobody else had been in the building. The night security guard had heard the explosion. By the time he reached the lab, there was nothing he could do. They hadn't let anybody see the body. What was left of it.

Bryn remembered how sometimes he used to come by· after school to meet his dad. He stood on this very spot watching the high guarded gates and waiting. Just like now. Bryn suddenly felt if he waited long enough, the gates might open, his father would walk out and everything would be normal again. As if the last few weeks had been a terrible nightmare.

A big, light-coloured car with darkened windows drew up at the kerb. The passenger window slid silently down. A man's voice beckoned him over. Bryn snapped out of his dream. He walked to the car, intrigued. Drivers of expensive motors didn't stop to ask directions. Especially

Zeta

That was easy-peasy, Kallie thought. Darya was such a wuzz. She believed everything Kallie told her. She was so happy when Kallie had asked her to be friends. Best friends, special friends. Kallie was popular, everybody wanted to be seen with her. She had long red curls and wore nice clothes. Kallie's pockets were always full of sweets. She had money to spend. Of course, Darya couldn't wait to ask her wonderful new friend home after school. Of course, Kallie wanted to see all round Darya's house. So Darya showed her round. The hallway, the kitchen, the living room. Then upstairs.

'This is my brother's room,' Darya said. She pointed to the closed door.

'My brother's a fat pig,' Kallie said and Darya had giggled delightedly. Kallie said such wonderfully funny things. Then they had both started grunting and pulling silly faces, like pigs.

'My brother's got a girlfriend,' Darya confided, 'guess who it is?' Kallie shook her head. 'It's that girl with the long black hair—you know, the one we saw this morning. I call her the witch girl. Do you think they kiss?'

Then Kallie had put her mouth close to Darya's ear and told her about boyfriends and girlfriends. Darya had listened, her eyes getting wider and wider with each disgusting revelation.

'Eugh!!' she exclaimed after Kallie had finished. 'I'm *never ever* going to have a boyfriend!'

After that, they played hide-and-seek. Kallie suggested

it. 'I *love* hide-and-seek,' she told Darya enthusiastically, 'I *never* get to play it at home, cos my brother's so fat, bits of him stick out when he hides.' At first, they'd hidden in easy places: behind doors, under tables. Then Kallie decided: 'Let's hide in really difficult places. You go first.' She had closed her eyes and started counting, 'One . . . two . . . three . . . ' As soon as Darya had left the room, Kallie opened her eyes, tiptoed after her and checked where Darya hid. Then on cat-silent feet, Kallie crept along the landing. She softly turned the handle of Bryn's door and went inside.

Bryn's room was not unlike Kirrin's: crammed with computer games and stuff. Kallie recognized the luridly coloured boxes that held Megatron 3, Galaxy Raiders, and Death Star. On the desk was a silver and blue Gamescom 9000—the same as Kirrin's. It was silent. A notice was pinned to the screen. She read it:

Another day done
All targets met
All systems fully operational
All customers satisfied
All staff keen and well motivated
All pigs fed and ready to fly.

Kallie frowned; she didn't get it. For a second or two, she experienced a feeling of mild panic. She didn't know what on earth she was looking for. She didn't know where it might be located and at any time she knew that Darya might get fed up hiding and come searching for her. Then, pulling herself together, Kallie concentrated and thought hard. Whenever she had anything to hide, she always put it in her top drawer, under her clothes. Nobody ever looked in there.

Kallie glided over to Bryn's chest of drawers. She slid open the top one, slipped her small hand inside and began rummaging around. At first she found nothing, then her fingers felt the edge of something hard. Kallie breathed quickly, her eyes sparkled. Carefully, so as not to disturb anything, she eased the object out from under Bryn's clothes. It was a small white plastic card. At one end there were some raised gold dots. Puzzled, Kallie looked at it. Funny. What was it for? Still, that wasn't her problem. Daddy would know all about it. She slipped the card into her pocket, pushed the drawer shut again. Then, as if she hadn't a care in the world, Kallie skipped downstairs, calling out: 'Ready or not, here I come!'

The car glided smoothly along the streets of the city. Bryn watched houses, front yards pass. He was strangely at ease. If this was what being kidnapped felt like, he thought, it was no big deal. They reached the outskirts of the city, where houses gave way to fields. The driver stopped the car, turned off the engine. He was a big man, dark hair silver-streaked. He wore a smart light-coloured summer suit and smelt of expensive cologne. 'Sorry to have to do that.' The driver held out a large gold-ringed hand. He had very clear blue eyes. 'Theo Laud. And you're Declan's son. You look just like him, you know.'

Bryn did a swift mental realignment. Not a kidnap. OK, that was good. He stared at the man. Recognized him. 'Hey, I've seen you somewhere before,' he exclaimed. 'You're famous, aren't you?'

The man looked amused. 'I'm one of the President's senior advisers, yes,' he nodded. 'I don't know whether that makes me famous. You might well have seen me on TV or in one of the newspapers.'

'That's it! The other day—you were being interviewed about something.' Bryn tried to remember what it was. And failed. He didn't really watch the news, it just filled the gap between shows he liked watching. He wasn't much interested in what was going on in the world—unless it had to do with sport.

'Yes, I'm always being interviewed about . . . something.' The man smiled wryly.

'And you knew my dad?'

'Oh yes. Very well.'

Bryn digested this fact. 'He never mentioned you.'

'No, I'm sure he didn't.'

'Why not?'

'Your father and I had . . . a rather unusual relationship.'

'Yeah?'

'That's why I'm here. He asked me to contact you sometime.'

'When did he ask you to do that?'

'He messaged me. Just before he . . . He wanted me to tell you . . . as much as we both thought you needed to know.'

'That's everything,' Bryn exclaimed.

Theo Laud gave a half-smile. 'That's a big demand, young friend. After all, what is "everything"—do you know? I don't think I do. And I'm probably a lot nearer to knowing it than most.'

'Huh?'

'Sorry, Bryn,' Laud apologized, 'force of habit. I'm a politician. We're trained not to answer direct questions.'

'OK,' Bryn said, 'so I just want to know about Dad. What happened. Why he died.'

'Yes, of course you do. And you shall. Only before I can tell you about that, I have to go back a little further. To when your father and I first met.' Laud leaned back into the pale fawn leather upholstery, stared out of the tinted front windscreen.

Bryn waited. He was on the edge of making a discovery. Maybe something that would help him understand what had gone wrong. Enable him to come to terms with his dad's death.

'I met Declan ten years ago,' Laud said, 'at a scientific conference. I was the visiting lecturer—that was before I became a government minister. Your father was there with a group from the Globechem factory. Anyway, we got talking during one of the breaks. And I liked him. I liked him immensely. It seemed to me that he had a logical mind, could think laterally. We started discussing the project I was working on—eco-regeneration. He understood the importance of it, suggested ways of proceeding, safeguards we'd need to introduce. I was impressed with his knowledge, his approach. So when the conference ended, we agreed to stay in touch, swap research data. We became scientific pen-pals, if you like.'

'He never mentioned you, ever,' Bryn said wonderingly.

'Maybe it wasn't that important. Not then. After all, we were just two colleagues, exchanging ideas. Afterwards, it was different. Then, my work began to be recognized. I was asked to help the government on various projects. I became the official scientific adviser.' He paused, 'and the rest is history, as they say.'

'And Dad?'

'We'd stopped corresponding by that time. My work had taken me into different areas. And then out of the blue, he got back in touch. He'd been working on a particular project, looking at the way various substances react to zero gravity. And one day he arrived at work to find all his research files had gone.'

'Gone?' Bryn queried. 'What do you mean "gone"?'

'They were no longer on his computer. Somebody had deleted them. Naturally, he reported it to his line manager. But, and this was the strange thing, he didn't seem worried. Nothing was done to retrieve the data. And that was the start of it. As time went on, Declan discovered other odd things—meetings held to which he wasn't invited. Areas of the factory that suddenly became "restricted access" only. Old and trusted staff started leaving, new people arriving. His work became more and more mundane until he was spending all his time copying out old files. He was being sidelined.'

'Why?'

'That was what he tried to find out. But nobody would answer his questions. He kept on asking awkward questions, taking it higher and higher up the chain. After all, he was a senior project manager, highly thought of. And then the threats began. He'd arrive at work to find his desk had been turned over—all his things were messed up or broken. Messages were left on his screen. Threatening messages.'

'Who from?'

'He couldn't trace them. But you know your father, he wasn't going to be bullied. It would take more than a few threats to stop him. So he went on probing, checking. Only now, he was more careful, watched his back. But he was still getting nowhere. And then one day, he found an old computer in a techno-store . . . '

'Ned.'

Laud laughed softly. 'Is that what he called it? Ned— yes, that's exactly the right name.'

'Sorry, I don't understand.' Bryn frowned.

'A long while ago,' Laud said, 'there used to be a group of people called Luddites. They tried to stop people taking their jobs away from them. They used to cause a lot of trouble. They smashed things up, refused to conform to the system. Their leader was called Ned Ludd.' He paused. 'I think that must have been in his mind. I like it. Anyway, as soon as he told me about Ned, I saw the potential. You see, Ned's a hacker—'

'Sorry?'

Laud sighed. 'There's so much you don't know. A hacker is a computer that is specifically programmed to

48

break into other computer systems. They were around in the first half of the century. Before all the computer companies merged and became Globecomp. Hackers were one-off machines, made exclusively for, or in some cases by, their owners. Each hacker was unique but they were all used for the same purpose—to get in where they weren't wanted and cause trouble.'

Laud continued to stare out of the window. 'It was hackers that caused the 2052 Cybercrash,' he said. 'They put viruses into the systems. When the viruses met up they produced a super virus for which there was no solution, no cure. Suddenly, every computer system throughout the globe crashed. Mankind lost everything in a couple of hours. Satellite communications, financial markets, historical records, everything we'd ever stored on computers vanished. And we never got it back. Not entirely. Even today, there are huge gaps in our knowledge. Areas that are completely blank.' He paused, pulled a wry face. 'Yes, all things considered, I reckon Ned's not a bad name for that machine of yours.'

'Dad used it to break into the computer system at Globechem, didn't he?'

'That's right. It took a few weeks to penetrate the system—they'd installed a firewall—but finally he got in.'

'And they killed him.' Bryn's hands tightened into fists. 'Some bastard killed him!'

'The official story was it was an accident,' Laud said evenly.

'Yeah, like you really believed that?' Bryn exclaimed.

'I thought it was . . . a bit of a coincidence,' Laud said.

'Right. How can you have an "accident" with a computer?'

'That thought crossed my mind too. But it seemed plausible. It could just have been true. Then I got your father's message.'

'He was set up, wasn't he?'

'Yes,' Laud said simply. He turned, looked into Bryn's face. 'Bryn, if I could have prevented it, I would have,' he said. He laid a hand on Bryn's shoulder. 'You have to believe me, I didn't want this to happen.'

'So what are you going to do about it?' Bryn asked.

'I'm going to find out who's behind it,' Laud said. 'That's what your father—what we both—want you to know.'

'And what is *it* then?' Bryn said, bitterly. 'What's the great big secret?'

'I don't know yet,' Laud answered. 'Not everything. It's something about research into a new type of rocket fuel. That much I have discovered. Which is strange in itself. We can't really afford to fund a space programme. There's still so much to do to restore the earth. There's some sort of new disease research just started too, though I'm not sure it's linked. What is interesting is that it's not just here—nearly all of the Globechem factories worldwide seem to be working on it. But for what purpose and who's authorizing it—that I don't know. Not yet. But I will, Bryn, believe me. And soon. Something's going on. And when good men like your father lose their lives, then it's something I intend to stop.'

Bryn sat in silence, staring at the digital display panel on the dashboard.

'Will you help me?' Laud asked.

'How?'

'Maybe I could borrow Ned; there are other systems I need to get into.'

'Sure.'

Laud handed him a small business card. 'That's my personal number and my private address. If you need to contact me about anything, don't hesitate.'

Bryn slid the card into his pocket. 'Thanks.'

'I'll take you back now.' Laud restarted the car. 'I'll be in touch, Bryn, I promise. Very soon. Your father was a personal friend; I'll see that he gets justice. You can trust me.'

'Right.' Bryn nodded.

Laud turned the car round. In silence, they headed back towards the city.

Eta

Bryn missed Kallie by nanoseconds. He got out of Theo Laud's car just as she scurried round the corner. Not that he'd have made any connections. Or cared if he had. Neots was just a teacher. Teachers inhabited a different planet. If they inhabited anywhere. He let himself into the house.

'Bryn!' Darya greeted him ecstatically.

'Hey, Da.' Bryn's mind was elsewhere. Trying to make sense of his meeting with Laud.

'Did you see her?' Da asked.

'Who?' How had his father become mixed up in this?

'My new friend Kallie. She just left.'

'That's nice, Da.'

'She's going to be my best friend.'

'Great.' Bryn nodded. Had he really promised Laud to lend Ned?

'Her dad's that teacher you don't like.'

'Uh-huh.' It was like a bad dream, all of it.

'We played some great games.'

'Mmmm.' Geez, he so badly wanted to talk it through with Dad.

Bryn went up to his room. Looked around. Everything was just as he'd left it. He tipped his bag out onto the floor and picked up his wallet. He opened it. There was a tiny picture of his dad inside. Bryn stared at the picture. Then, inspiration hit. He flipped open Ned's lid. A fanfare, which seemed to go on slightly longer than before, was followed by loud applause and cheering. The computer was turning megalomania into an art form.

'Hey, Ned.' Bryn slid into his seat.

'I am yours to command,' the voice said grandly. Bryn just knew it didn't mean it.

'Great.' He held up the picture. 'Scan,' he commanded. Ned transferred the picture neatly on to the screen. It was still very tiny.

'Can you magnify?' There was a pause. The picture slowly grew until it filled the whole screen.

Yes!! Why hadn't he thought of this before?

'Hey, Dad,' Bryn said. 'We need to talk.'

The Head of Security disliked Mr Neots. Disliked him very much. He did not appreciate being told how to do his job by some self-appointed busybody masquerading as a teacher. Mr Tight-Arse, he called him. That was on a good day. So it was with very little goodwill that he faced Mr Neots over his desk on the fourth floor of Globecop HQ (mission statement: One people, one purpose). He had been hoping to get home early, put his feet up. Now he wasn't going to. All because this rat-faced patsy claimed to have uncovered a breach of security.

He remembered ruefully that his astrological prediction for today had said beware of timewasters.

The Head of Security leant his elbows on his desk, rested his chin with exaggerated weariness upon his hands. Above the desk was the laser-imaged likeness of the President, his benign elderly features also staring down with a parallel world-weary expression. There, however, the resemblance ended. The Head of Security had a swarthy, heavy-jowled face. He looked like a pugilistic bulldog. Right now, he was a bulldog who badly wanted to be somewhere else.

'Yeah?' he grunted, deliberately staring at a spot just left of Mr Neots's head.

Mr Neots was not intimidated. Moronic thug, he thought to himself. Bog-stupid cretin. Just like the man in the last place. He drew from his leather attaché case a small white plastic card with gold dots at one end. He placed it carefully on the desk.

'Very nice, squire,' the Head of Security said. 'First year art class been busy, have they? Hardly seems like a big security risk to me.'

'Do you know what this is?' Mr Neots asked.

'No, but I'm sure you're going to tell me.'

'It's a calling card.'

'Right. A calling card.'

You are a mindless robotic imbecile, Mr Neots thought. He sighed. 'Let me explain it to you,' he said with exaggerated politeness. 'Calling cards are used—or rather, were used—by certain individuals to send messages of a dubious and illegal nature to each other.'

'They'd have to write small,' the Head of Security observed brightly.

'They are for use in a computer.' Mr Neots wondered what the punishment was for striking a Globecop official.

'Ah. *Computer* cards. Got you now. Why didn't you say that in the first place?'

Mr Neots ground his teeth but continued to smile. Asinine goon, he thought. Oafish lackbrain.

'So then, let me get it straight,' the Head of Security said slowly, fully aware of the effect he was having and enjoying it. 'This calling card represents a breach of security. And you want me to do what? Arrest it?'

'I want you to take this matter seriously,' Mr Neots snapped, his control finally going. 'This card comes from the home of one of my pupils. It was found by my eight-year-old daughter who, knowing her duty, brought it straight to me.'

So the nasty little brat has been poking her nose into other people's business again, the Head of Security thought silently, tell me about it!

'You do know that it's against the law to possess something like this?' Mr Neots said. 'I refer you to the Official Secrets Act of 2053, subsection 44, paragraph iii. I want this boy watched and followed. I want you to prepare a full report on his movements.'

'Yeah, yeah.' The Head of Security was unimpressed. Follow a kid round all day? On your bike, mate, he thought.

'And there are others in the same class. I think you should watch them too. Especially one girl. It seems that she has started going round with the boy. She is very odd in her behaviour.'

'I thought they were all odd at that school, squire,' the Head of Security commented drily.

'Bright. They're bright. It's a school for bright pupils,' Mr Neots snapped. 'Only sometimes they're a little too bright for their own good.'

The Head of Security drew a pad and a pencil towards him. 'OK. Give me their names and addresses and I'll get one of my men on to it tomorrow.'

Mr Neots carefully repeated the names. The Head of Security wrote them down, breathing heavily as he did so. Then he reached out to take the card, but Mr Neots was too quick for him. Like a serpent striking its prey, his long bony fingers reached out and grabbed it.

'Oh no,' he said smoothly, putting the card in his pocket, 'I'm afraid I can't leave this with you. There are others who may well be interested in it. Others, may I say without mentioning any names, who are in the *higher* echelons of government. Maybe even the highest level of all,' he added, nodding significantly. 'So you understand how important it is that you do your duty, don't you? I mean, you wouldn't want it to reach those in authority that you neglected to follow up this meeting. Would you?'

Bryn felt better. Much better. It was amazing how talking things through had cleared his mind, focused his thoughts. He felt level, grounded, almost back to normal.

'Thanks, Ned,' he said.

'I live to serve.'

'Whatever.'

'Do you want me to shut down now?' the metallic voice asked hopefully.

'No, not quite yet.'

A sound like a resigned sigh seemed to come from the black box. Bryn ignored it. He activated the Gamescom. 'As you've been so helpful,' he grinned, 'I'm going to teach you how to play Megatron 3.'

Theta

Jade woke up. Behind her closed eyelids, she could see sunshine streaming in. Another hot summer day. Another opportunity to reconnect to the human race. Or not. Jade got up and prepared herself for the day ahead. Humming tunelessly, she showered, air-dried her hair. She picked out some weekend clothes. She decided that today was going to be a good day, so it would be. Jade believed in the power of perception over reality. Sooner or later it had to work.

Outside the house, the watcher waited. People went by. They failed to notice him. That was how it should be. The watcher's refractive clothes rendered him practically invisible. Nobody saw him standing in the shadows. Nobody ever did. But Jade could perceive things that didn't exist in the normal continuum of space and time. She could see things that were and were not and were yet to come into being. Within seconds of leaving the house, she spotted him.

At first, Jade didn't connect the watcher with herself. She had no reason to. But it quickly became apparent that she was the focus of his attention. Jade started to duck and dive. In and out of alleyways, up walkways, weaving around cars. She tried her best to shake him off. But the watcher was a professional. He was trained to follow. He stayed with her.

Kirrin was determined to talk to Bryn. He'd tried all week, but school was an impossible place. Too big, too many distractions. Now it was Sunday. Kirrin knew exactly where Bryn would be—down at the Gamesmart. It was where they all went, the compoheads, to swap ideas, try the new games on offer. He decided to check it out.

The Gamesmart was heaving with customers. The air resonated bleeps, electronic music, and flashing lights. Bryn was there, on his own, trying out the latest game when Kirrin walked into the store. Boldly, Kirrin went straight over. 'That looks like a good game,' he said. Bryn looked up from the screen. The fat red-haired kid again, he thought, frowning slightly. What was it with him?

'Try it,' he said politely, surrendering his console. He wandered off towards the display racks.

'Oh, thanks,' Kirrin stuttered. This was so not what he wanted to happen. He played the game for a couple of minutes, to show willing. Then he gave the console to a group of younger boys, went in search of Bryn once more. He found him studying the rows of Megatron boxes.

'Are you going to get a game?' Kirrin asked.

'Might do.' Bryn picked up Megatron 4, turned it over and read the blurb on the back.

'Wow! You must be really good,' Kirrin said admiringly. 'I've only got as far as Level 12 on Megatron 3.'

'Mmm.' Bryn was actually thinking of buying the game for Ned not for himself. He wasn't telling Kirrin this, though. Having a computer addicted to computer games was just the latest of his various problems.

'Maybe you could show me how to get to your level some time?' Kirrin suggested hopefully.

'Maybe.' Bryn shrugged non-committally, went to pay for his game. Kirrin's heart leaped for joy. Finally, he'd broken through. He rewarded himself with a sweet from the crumpled bag in his pocket.

Bryn joined a long line at the paypoint. It stretched out into the mall, but was moving steadily. Suddenly, there was a commotion behind him. A warning cry followed by a crash. Bryn turned. A girl, black hair flying, had collided with one of the carousel racks. Boxes of Toxic Avenger spilled all over the walkway. The girl scrambled to her feet. Her face was poppy red, eyes wild and staring. She didn't stop to pick up the mess. Instead, she ran straight on down the walkway.

'Did you recognize her?' Kirrin came up behind Bryn. Bryn shook his head. 'It was that girl from your class,' Kirrin told him, 'you know, the funny one. What's her name?'

'Jade,' Bryn said. He thrust the Megatron 4 box into Kirrin's arms. 'Here. You take this. I have to go.'

Jade was running out of breath and ideas. Being followed by the watcher was like getting a zit: the more she tried to get rid of him, the more persistently he was there. She ran through the mall, leaving a trail of debris. The watcher stayed behind her. She headed home. The watcher never left her. By the time she reached her estate, Jade felt as if her lungs were on fire. Her eyes were streaming, her legs ached. And the watcher was still on her case.

Suddenly, Jade lost her temper. This was supposed to be her lovely day. And she'd spent most of it trying to shake off some thug who'd taken it into his mindless head to stalk her. Furiously, she advanced upon the watcher, teeth bared, eyes shooting fire. 'Frakk off, you zeek!' she shouted. She stamped hard on his foot. There was a yell of pain followed by loud swearing. Jade turned and fled into the house.

Then, just as suddenly, her adrenalin went. She started shaking. What had possessed her? She had just made a seriously stupid mistake. What was she—crazy? The guy had looked big and mean. Right now, he was probably calling for back-up. Jade wasn't sure what would happen when the back-up arrived, but she guessed it wasn't going to be a party in the park. Possibly it might involve pain of some sort. A lot of pain. Maybe she was going to die . . .

Jade locked and double-bolted the front door. She went round the house checking that all the windows were firmly shut. She made completely sure that the whole place was virtually impregnable. Then, clutching the largest and sharpest kitchen knife she could find, she crouched behind the sofa and waited.

When Bryn knocked on the front door, Jade's first reaction was to leap out of her hiding place and run. Bryn knocked again. Jade crept to the front door. Dry-mouthed, she called out hoarsely, 'Go away! I've got a knife.'

'It's me,' Bryn said.

Jade unlocked and opened the door.

'Did you say *knife*?' Bryn stared at her incredulously. Jade closed the door behind him. She felt her face going bright red with embarrassment. 'Er . . . it's nothing,' she mumbled. 'You know, just kidding around some.' She slid the knife behind her back and dropped it through the bannister rails.

'Look, are you OK?' Bryn asked anxiously.

'Yeah, fine,' Jade lied. 'Why?'

'Only I thought I might have seen you at the mall.'

'Me? I've been here all day.'

'You were running. Pretty fast. Like you were being chased by someone.'

'Did you see anyone chasing?'

'No.'

'Couldn't have been me then.' Jade shook her head.

The logic of this escaped Bryn. Still, she looked all right. 'So . . . you're OK,' he repeated slowly.

Jade nodded. She thought fast. They wouldn't come for her with Bryn here. Too risky. She glanced at her watch. Her parents would be back later. She hoped. 'Umm. . . . you doing anything?' she asked, trying to keep the edge of fear and panic out of her voice.

'Not much.'

'Want to listen to some music?'

'Go on then.' Bryn followed her into the shiny-bright white living room.

A couple of hours later, Bryn left the house. He felt good. For the first time, he thought, he and Jade had talked. Really talked. It had been OK, though he didn't think much of her taste in music. The fat red-haired kid must have got it wrong. It couldn't have been Jade at the mall. He was just a stupid junkbrain, Bryn decided, pulling a face. Couldn't see straight. There was nothing wrong with Jade. She was fine.

Jade stood in the shelter of the curtain. She saw Bryn go. As if at a given signal, two watchers stepped silently out of the shadows. With a shudder, Jade recognized one. They glanced back at the house, appeared to confer briefly. Jade waited, scarcely daring to breathe. Then, to her relief, they turned and walked quickly after Bryn.

Kirrin bought the Megatron 4 game, deciding that if he tried really hard maybe he'd reach the first level by the time he saw Bryn again. That'd give him something positive to talk about. Years of living with his parents had made Kirrin sensitive: he realized Bryn wasn't really interested in him. But Kirrin also sensed that Bryn was too nice to knock him back. The cruelty of his father was not part of Bryn's personality. He didn't get pleasure out of hurting people.

So, doggedly, Kirrin stuck to his plan. It was more than obeying his father. Now Kirrin was on a mission. A personal quest. Bryn was the nearest he'd ever come to having a friend. He desperately wanted to keep the relationship going. OK it wasn't much, as friendships went. However, given whose son he was, it was a whole lot better than nothing.

Kirrin carried the game upstairs. Sundays were no good. He tried to stay in his room, emerging occasionally for food and drink. Sometimes, he managed to lay in stocks of food and drink. Then he didn't emerge until Monday. Kirrin liked school. It got him out of the house. Today, he had no stocks of food. And he was hungry after his long walk home. He went down to raid the fridge.

In the bleak, cold kitchen, he found his parents sitting at the table in icy silence. There was a half-empty gin bottle on the table. His mother stared moodily into a glass. His father was reading the paper. He looked up quickly as Kirrin entered.

'Ah yes . . . Kirrin,' he said slowly. Kirrin was sure his father forgot his name sometimes.

'I've been out.'

'Indeed. And now you are back.' Kirrin hated it when his father spoke in that sharp-slicing voice.

'Did you have a nice time?' his mother asked listlessly. She tilted the glass, watching the colourless liquid flow from side to side. Kirrin nodded. 'I was with Bryn,' he said casually. The announcement had the desired effect. His father immediately put down the paper. His eyes became hooded and watchful. 'We went to the Gamesmart,' Kirrin continued, helping himself from the fridge. 'I bought a new game. We're going to try it next week.'

'Good. Good.' Mr Neots nodded approvingly.

Kirrin loaded himself up with food. 'I'm going to my room to practise now,' he said, backing out of the kitchen.

'Yes, why don't you do that.' Mr Neots gave Kirrin a reptilian smile. He picked up the paper again. His mother unscrewed the bottle, poured the rest of it into her glass. Her hand shook as she raised the glass to her mouth. Kirrin fled.

Bryn saw the flyer on his way home from Jade's. It was pinned neatly to a noticeboard. He read it, then checked it a second time, just to be sure:

Globechem Open Day
Saturday July 21st from 10.30 a.m.
Come and see Science in Action.
Fun activities all day. Admission free.

Then, in slightly smaller letters he read:

Opening Ceremony to be performed by:
Professor Theodore Laud, M.Sc. D.Phil.
Senior Science Adviser.
Globechem. One planet, one purpose

Coincidence? Bryn didn't think so. Laud must have decided to check things out for himself. Bryn unpinned the flyer, folded it and put it in his pocket. Ever since his dad's death, he'd wanted to get inside Globechem. To see the actual area where his dad had worked. Now, he'd got a valid excuse. Bryn had things he wanted to check out too, important things. Sure he trusted Theo Laud. But Laud had his own agenda—discovering who was behind the secret research, finding out what was going on and why. Bryn felt instinctively that this was Laud's primary motivation. His dad was secondary. Bryn understood.

Laud was a top-ranking politician, he had a big global agenda. Bryn's agenda could be summed up in three words: get the killer.

Mr Neots folded the paper, circled the article about the Open Day with a pen. He couldn't believe his luck. Things were beginning to move, to stir. At long last. He'd waited so very patiently. Waited and worked. A little bit here, a little bit there. Prying into this, reporting upon that. Getting his name known. Now it was starting to happen. In his briefcase he had a letter of introduction from his government contact. He'd worked hard for it. Now here was a golden opportunity to use it.

Professor Theodore Laud, senior science adviser, he thought. What Laud had done, he could do too. Yes. He was born for high office. If everything went to plan, he'd soon be quitting his mundane job, this lacklustre marriage. Soon, he'd be on his way to the top. Maybe right to the very top. And why not? After all, wasn't it the place where he rightly belonged?

Iota

'This is truly weird,' Gil said. He shook his head disbelievingly.

'You get used to it,' Bryn told him. Jade stared out of the window. Rain was coming down in slanted silver sheets. First for weeks, she thought. She listened to the sound of falling rain drumming rhythmically on Bryn's windowsill. She was content.

'Hey, look, it's reached the final level,' Gil exclaimed.

'Uh-oh wait for it . . . ' Bryn warned.

There was a triumphant fanfare of trumpets followed by a chorus of voices chanting: 'Yes . . . *yes* . . . YES!!!'

'How can a computer play games all by itself?' Gil asked.

'Beats me,' Bryn said. He put Megatron 3 back in its box, loaded CyberBandits. 'OK, Ned, try this one.'

Gil stared at him in disbelief. 'You talk to it?'

'Err . . . ' Bryn felt his face going red. 'No, of course not. Just kidding around, hey.'

The computer started making 'how interesting' sounds as it investigated the new game. Gil watched it closely. 'And you say your dad found it in the techno-store?' he asked.

'Yeah.' Now he'd got past the ego-as-big-as-the-universe syndrome and the multiple personality disorder, Bryn decided he quite liked Ned. Especially since playing computer games had taken over its life. He felt they'd finally got something in common.

'Does it do anything else?' Gil asked, watching Ned's screen flicker.

'No, that's all it does,' Bryn lied.

'Bit boring.'

'It seems happy enough,' Bryn said, deliberately misunderstanding.

Gil gave him a funny look. Jade continued staring dreamily out of the window. She'd seen Ned earlier, before Gil arrived. To Jade, computers were just boxes that did stuff. They didn't interest her.

'Is she all right?' Gil lowered his voice, jerked his head in her direction.

'She's fine.'

'What's she doing round here?'

'Just visiting.'

Gil sighed. So much about Bryn had changed since his dad died. First there was digging the hole—which had been discovered by his mum, as Gil predicted it would be. They'd had to fill it all in, which took ages because Bryn had insisted on turning it into a kind of funeral ceremony. He'd buried a whole load of his dad's tools. Some of them brand new. It was crazy, Gil told him. Wasteful. They'd had a row about it. Bryn had barely spoken to him for a while. Now he'd taken up with the class oddball. Gil's loyalty was being pushed to its limit. 'Geez, I can't believe it's only Wednesday,' he sighed. 'This week's dragging. Weekend feels miles away.'

Bryn got up, unpinned the flyer from his bulletin board. He gave it to Gil. 'That reminds me—I picked this up the other day. You interested?'

Gil glanced at the flyer. Then he looked at Bryn.

'You're not serious?'

'Why?'

'Mate, you don't want to go back there. Think about it. That was where your . . . where . . . ' Gil's voice tailed off awkwardly.

'Where my dad died. You can say it.'

Jade turned, started watching their interaction.

'Right. So why go back? Only stir things up all over again.'

'Because I have to.' Bryn spoke decisively. 'Can't you see? I need to see it again, maybe talk to some of his old team if they're around. Somebody might have noticed something.'

'Noticed what?' Gil queried. 'He was on his own when it happened. It was an accident.'

Bryn closed his mouth firmly. Already he'd said too much. There was silence whilst he and Gil stared at each other. Then Gil lowered his eyes, groaned. 'Are you sure about this?'

'Yeah.' Bryn nodded. 'So, are you in?'

Gil sighed. 'Well, I think you're crazy, but I suppose somebody'd better go with you to keep an eye on you. Yeah, I'll come.'

'Great. What about you?' Bryn asked Jade.

'Where're you going?'

Gil handed her the flyer. Jade read it concentratedly. 'Professor Theodore Laud,' she murmured. 'Senior Science Adviser. He's got a lot of letters after his name, hasn't he?'

'He's a brilliant scientist,' Gil told her. Bryn said nothing. 'I've seen him on TV. This guy's so respected even the President listens to him,' Gil went on. 'You can't get better than that.'

'A small bag of fries is better than the President,' Jade announced unexpectedly.

Gil rolled his eyes, made 'I told you' faces at Bryn, but Bryn didn't notice. Jade's bizarre words had struck a sudden chord. He'd heard them before. When? Bryn scanned back. Muck-up day last term. A boy in class had written *A small bag of fries is better than nothing. Nothing is better than the President. Therefore a small bag of fries is better than the President.* He'd sent it round the learning screens. A joke. They'd all laughed. Ha ha. Then Mr Neots had come into the room, read the message. The laughter had stopped abruptly.

Soon after that, the boy had disappeared. He'd not been to school since. What was his name? Funny that he should think of him now, Bryn thought. He tried to remember whether the boy had changed school or what. He seemed to have just vanished without trace. Still, it happened; people moved on. Nothing to get major stressed about. He grinned at Jade.

'Hey, don't let old Neots hear you say things like that,' he joked. 'Remember . . . you know . . . whatsisname?'

The President was very old. Nobody knew his exact age, his real name. He was a mysterious figure who had been in office for so long that nobody could remember a time when he wasn't there. He spoke with wisdom and knowledge. He was old and wise and revered. Not loved— it was not possible to love someone as remote and distant.

But if you asked anybody on any street of any city, they would tell you unhesitatingly that with the President in control of everything, war had been abolished, crime eliminated, and everyone lived contentedly. And if you relayed that message back to the President, you would see a smile cross his thin lips as he nodded in agreement. It was only what he expected. After all, he had spent a long time creating this world for his people to live in.

The President sat in his office, reading a report that had just been placed upon his desk. These reports were his only link with the outside world. In the seclusion of his room, he could think and meditate. He could work out his global strategies undisturbed. He felt no need for human contact; he hadn't done so for a very very long time. Solitude. That was how he liked it.

Not that the President wanted to be an entirely remote figure. He needed people to be able to relate to him. That was why his profile appeared on every item sold by GlobeCo and its subsidiaries, companies he founded and owned and controlled.

Today, the screens that made up the walls of his office were filled with images of a tropical forest. Green leaves waved gently in the warm breeze, monkeys leaped and chattered. Rainbow-coloured birds swooped and called. In real life, of course, there were no forests. They had all been chopped down or burned long ago. But thanks to virtual reality, whole forests could now be created by computer. They were frequently shown on TV as examples of how GreenGlobe (Mission statement: One planet, one purpose) was successfully regenerating the world. The images were so lifelike nobody realized that they were false. The same company created rain and wind and snow as the seasons dictated. Only, of course, there were no actual seasons, just artificially manufactured ones, but they were so realistic that nobody was aware they were fake.

The President picked up the memo, stared down at it. A boy, he thought in disgust. A stupid boy. How much could he possibly know? He was supposed to be exceptionally bright, but how bright was he? There was something familiar about that surname though . . . had he heard it before? He scanned the report again: Neots—he certainly recognized that name. The man had submitted many useful reports. He was clearly loyal and efficient. Unlike most of the government watchers and informers, who couldn't locate a misdemeanour if it jumped up and bit them. Maybe it was time he encouraged this Neots. Let him know his efforts had not gone unnoticed. After all, he would need men like that.

When the time came.

The President placed the tips of his fingers together, leaned his elbows upon the desk.

'So it begins,' he murmured.

He closed his eyes and tried to relax. Make your mind a complete blank, he told himself. Forget everything. Most of all forget that you were once, a very, very long time ago, a clever young research graduate at a top university. Forget that you had an equally clever friend who was a scientist. Who one day cracked the human DNA code— the genetic blueprint of the human race. Forget that this friend developed an experimental drug that worked upon the ageing gene $-p21$, stopping the body from wearing out.

The friend was long dead and his revolutionary drug had been discredited and passed into the mists of scientific obscurity.

But the result of his experiment lived on.

Kappa

Music played and flags waved in the breeze. Smiling workers handed out brightly coloured balloons, each bearing the familiar Globechem logo. Tubs of coloured flowers lined the way to the main entrance. Hugely gross, Jade thought to herself. Overhead, an immense silver airship hovered in the sky, trailing the words 'Welcome to Globechem Open Day'.

Jade stood in line, waiting for the gates to open. She guessed Bryn and Gil were somewhere way up front. She'd meant to make the 10 o'clock meet time, but had overslept.

Around her, people chatted, children laughed and played. Jade wondered why they were here, what they expected to see. A smartly dressed employee came down the line holding a big bunch of balloons. Kids screamed and pushed in their eagerness to get one. 'D'ya want a balloon?' the man held a string out towards her. Jade withered him with a look. 'Hey, please yourself.' The man shrugged his shoulders, passed on down the line.

There was a noise to the rear of the waiting crowd. A big light-coloured car with darkened windows was moving swiftly towards the barriers. People skittered out of the way. Two black-leather-clad motorcycle outriders rode on either side of the car, then came together in front as the barriers were raised to let it enter. Inside the car, the big man leaned forward in his seat, peering out of the window. His dark hair was streaked with silver. He scanned the people in the crowd as if he was looking for one specific individual. The car shot through the barrier and came to a halt by the entrance. The man sat back, a thoughtful expression upon his face. For a moment, he remained motionless. Then he opened his briefcase, took out the prepared speech of welcome, and waited for his driver to open the door.

Further along the line, Kirrin fidgeted uncomfortably. He was wearing a white shirt and long black trousers. They were itchy and hot. He'd wanted to wear casual clothes but he wasn't allowed to. This was a special event. He and Kallie were on show. The happy Neots family enjoying an interesting day out together. Except that they weren't and this wasn't. Kirrin was so not interested in going round Globechem. He would have given anything to stay home in his room playing on his computer—he'd nearly reached level 2 of his new game. Instead, he'd been bundled into his best clothes and forced to accompany his father and sister. He glanced surreptitiously at his watch. Maybe there'd be a canteen, he thought, with good snacks. Kirrin sighed sadly. It was an awfully long time since breakfast.

Kallie Neots jiggled up and down delightedly. She'd got three balloons, more than the kids around her had. And she was wearing her pretty dress, the blue flowered one. And her hair was tied up in blue ribbons. She was a little princess. Daddy had said so. Kallie was happy. She loved being admired; Daddy's friends always admired her. Today Daddy was going to meet some very important friends. Kallie was going to help him by smiling sweetly and being a good girl. Then Daddy would give her a present for being so special. If only Kirrin wasn't here, she thought, frowning. Spoiling things as usual. Hateful Kirrin. Kallie slyly shot out her foot, and gave him a sharp kick on the shins.

'Ow!' Kirrin yelled.

Mr Neots turned on him. 'Can't you stand still?' he snapped angrily.

Kirrin cowered under his father's gaze. 'Sorry,' he mumbled.

Kallie opened her eyes wide, smiled her sweetest smile. 'Are we going in now, Daddy?' she asked in her cute-little-girl voice.

'Soon,' her father said, stroking her red curls. 'Not long now. Are you looking forward to it, my princess?'

Kallie squeezed her father's hand. 'Yes, Daddy,' she smiled, 'of course I am. Ever so much.'

At the front of the queue, Bryn and Gil watched the Globechem head honchos line up for a photocall. They all looked identical: tall middle-aged men with sharp faces and even sharper suits. Bryn scanned along the line. Who had decided to pull the plug on his father? The one at the end? The one in the middle—it was impossible to tell. Maybe they were all in on it. A global conspiracy. That was what Laud had hinted at.

'Hey, this must be the famous prof.,' Gil murmured as the car and its two outriders pulled up. The driver opened the rear door and Laud emerged, looking exactly as Bryn recollected him. There was a spattering of applause from the crowd. Laud was miked up by a Globechem minion. The music rose to a crescendo, then stopped. Silence fell. Laud stepped forward and started to speak.

Jade met up with Bryn and Gil in the entrance. The crowds surged around them, heading for the various visitor attractions. Everything was clearly labelled, but the smartly dressed receptionist behind the desk was busy fielding enquiries. Every now and then she gave the two boys a suspicious glance.

'Sorry,' Jade said briefly. Then she muttered disgustedly: 'Plastic flowers.'

'Huh?'

'In the tubs. Plastic flowers.' Jade wrinkled her nose. 'Totally acrid.' She peered at the people going by. So many pink blobby faces, she thought. Their eyes so stupidly eager. Their mouths opening and shutting like stranded goldfish. Jade shuddered. She was not a crowd person.

'Come on.' Bryn pulled her by the elbow. 'Let's go and look round.'

Jade and Gil followed him along the main corridor. Through the open plan office with empty desks and blank computer screens. They crossed an outdoor area where some clowns were entertaining a group of little kids, walked towards a block labelled 'Research and Development'. Bryn pushed open the door.

'This was where my dad worked,' he said.

And it was the same as he remembered. Same cluttered workbenches filled with glass dishes and rows of test-tubes. Same bank of computers flashing numbers. Same white-coated figures moving quietly around checking, noting, feeding data into the computers.

But it was not the same. For starters, there was a different name over the door at the far end that led to his dad's office. There was shatterproof glass screening partitioning off the work area from the rest of the building. A sign saying Restricted Access. And the white-coated people were not his father's old team. They were total strangers. He'd never seen any of them before. Even the posters on the walls had been changed. Bryn stared. Then he leaned his forehead against the cold impersonal glass. He hadn't expected this. He felt shocked, dismayed. He had not anticipated that all traces of his dad and his work had been completely removed.

Kirrin sat on a bench, munching a doughnut. He'd managed to become separated from his father and his sister. He licked sugar off his fingers and sighed contentedly. He had the two things that made him happy: food and the absence of his family. To these, he added a third: he got his Minicom out and began playing a game. Soon, he was completely absorbed, focusing upon the tiny screen, his fingers pressing the buttons. After a while, some smaller boys came over, sat down and started playing games as well. With a bit of luck, Kirrin thought, his father would forget about him until it was time to go.

Bryn felt as if he'd been hit in the stomach. First Globechem had eradicated his father. Now they'd eradicated his workplace too. And got rid of everybody connected with him. Why? Bryn knew there was only one man who could tell him. He had to see Laud. Somehow, he had to break through the security cordon that surrounded him. They needed to talk.

He felt a touch on his arm. 'OK, mate?' Gil sounded concerned. 'You've gone a bit white.'

Bryn dragged his mind back from the black hole it was sinking into. 'I'm fine,' he muttered.

'Bit of a shock, seeing it again?'

'Yeah. Bit of a shock. That's right.'

'Want to get a drink and sit down?'

Bryn nodded. He needed to collect his thoughts, get a grip on his feelings, work out a plan. They went to the canteen. Gil got three cans from the drinks dispenser. They sat down at a table. Jade peeled back the lid of her drink, looked around. Then she stiffened. Her mouth set in a tight line. 'Look over there,' she whispered, pointing. Bryn and Gil turned round. At a table by the window sat Laud, surrounded by Globechem bosses. Hovering by them, an ingratiating smile upon his face and clutching a small red-haired girl by the hand, was Mr Neots.

'What's *he* doing here?' Jade hissed.

'Same as us.' Gil sipped his drink calmly.

'Ignore him,' Bryn told her. 'Just pretend he doesn't exist.'

But Jade couldn't. She sat ramrod straight in her chair, throat dry. Her heart started pounding. Fear, terror: it was right here in the room. And it was so strong. Why was she the only one to feel it? Jade tore her gaze away from Neots, who'd now pulled up a chair and joined the group at the far table. The red-haired child was sitting on his lap, simpering at Professor Laud. Jade tried to concentrate upon her drink, the boys, the pattern on the floor, anything to take her mind away from what she was hearing in her head: the desperate and abandoned cries, the sound of horses galloping, the noise of battle, screams of dying men. The terrifying sense that everything familiar and known and loved was going, was being destroyed. Bryn and Gil seemed oblivious to what was happening to her. Words started to form in Jade's head. Jagged, cruel words. She clapped her hands over her mouth. Finally, she could stand no more. She jumped up, her chair falling over, and ran out of the canteen.

Mr Neots congratulated himself. The meeting had been a resounding success. Better than he could ever have hoped. Nothing had gone wrong. From the moment Laud had looked up, met his eye, beckoned him over, to the moment he'd got up, Laud's private number folded in a scrap of paper in his pocket. And what a meeting it had been! For the first time, Mr Neots had been encouraged to expand upon his ideas. And the professor had listened. Really listened. He'd never taken his eyes from Mr Neots's face. Shrewd blue eyes that seemed to search into his very soul. As if he knew what Mr Neots was saying behind the words. As if he looked right inside him, saw the deep, important things that were hidden from everyone else.

It was astonishing. Mr Neots felt as if he and the famous professor had known each other for years. They'd spoken together like old friends. Nobody else had managed to get near Laud, Mr Neots thought. Just him. He'd been singled out. Yes, that was it exactly, singled out. Great things were surely going to follow. He was convinced of it. He was on his way up.

'Are we going home now?' Kallie piped.

Mr Neots smiled tenderly down at her. 'If you want to,' he said.

'Did I help you, Daddy?'

'You were perfect, my treasure. A real little helper.'

'Kirrin didn't help, did he?'

A scowl crossed Mr Neots's aquiline features. 'No,' he said shortly. 'I think we can safely say your brother was, as usual, no help whatsoever.'

'Are we going to find him, Daddy?'

Mr Neots took her hand in his. 'Maybe Kirrin deserves to walk home, what do you think?'

Kallie nodded. She giggled delightedly. 'Oohh, yes. It'll take him ages,' she exclaimed. 'And it's started raining too.'

Jade was furious with herself. Yet again, she'd spoilt things. Even though she'd come back, explained her sudden flight away by saying she'd eaten something that disagreed with her, she sensed a cooling in the atmosphere. Bryn barely spoke after that. He walked round withdrawn and remote. Gil tried a few half-hearted attempts at conversation, then gave up too. Jade cursed her stupidity. Everything was going so well. She'd been accepted. Now she felt alone, once more the outsider looking in.

They tramped round the complex in silence, finally arriving back at the front steps just as the big light-coloured car was pulling up. The driver got out, opened the rear door. Professor Laud and his entourage appeared in the entrance. Suddenly, Bryn ran forward. The two minders grabbed him. He said something to Laud, who was looking at him, alarmed. Then Laud barked a curt order. The men released him and to Jade and Gil's astonishment, Laud beckoned Bryn over to him. They stood a little apart, talking in low voices. Eventually Bryn returned to the others. He was walking very slowly, staring back, not taking his eyes off Laud, who got straight into the car and was driven swiftly away. Bryn watched him go. He seemed dazed, shaken.

'Hey,' Gil said, 'what was all that about?'

'I had to talk to him,' Bryn said dully.

'Man, you can't just do that. He's famous.'

'It's OK. He knows me, I met him once before.'

'You met Professor Laud?' Gil exclaimed.

'Yeah,' Bryn said, 'and that's how I know . . . ' he paused, hesitated, bit his lip.

'You know what?'

'I know that man wasn't him,' Bryn said.

Lambda

It had been a spur of the moment decision. All morning, the frustration had grown. A sense of helplessness. He'd hoped for so much, perhaps too much. Bryn knew his expectations were unrealistic—even if he could have talked to some of his father's old colleagues, it was unlikely they'd have told him anything he didn't already know. Still, he'd gone on hoping.

Then everything started to go wrong. The lab had been glassed off. There were no colleagues to be seen anywhere. Bryn's hopes had been dashed. The day began to slide sideways with alarming alacrity. Bryn had tried to contact Laud but the crowd around him had been too big. Now Laud was leaving. Bryn saw his last opportunity fading away. So he'd taken drastic action.

At first, Laud had been surprised, perhaps a bit shaken. After all, Bryn could have been carrying a knife, anything. Then, Bryn reminded him who he was, when they'd met. And Laud had calmed down, taken him aside, let him speak. But Bryn sensed at once that it wasn't like before. There wasn't the same easy flow between them. He kept on having to prompt Laud—as if he'd completely forgotten their last meeting. Bryn had to remind him about the connection with his father, the secret research, how his dad had died in the freak 'accident'. It was a weird feeling. Laud was standing right in front of him, but at the same time he wasn't there at all.

Gradually Bryn felt the conversation floundering. Laud glanced at his watch, started moving away. The security men stopped fidgeting. Bryn desperately wanted to prolong the meeting. He hadn't told Laud half the stuff he needed to. Then he remembered Ned. Laud was interested in Ned. So he'd said to Laud, jokingly, 'You'll never guess what Ned's got into.' He was intending to tell Laud about the strange machine's addiction to computer games. Bryn thought it'd amuse him, remind him of their former chat. And Laud had half-smiled, looked away and said carelessly: 'Ah yes, Ned. Tell me again—he's your brother isn't he?'

That was when Bryn knew something was very wrong. He stared straight into Laud's face and suddenly saw him for the first time. He noticed that Laud's skin was too smooth, too shiny, as if it wasn't skin at all, but some sort of skin substitute. His hair was too immaculately groomed, each strand in place, like a wig. To his amazement, Bryn realized he was looking into the eyes of a total stranger. For a second or two, he was completely thrown. He didn't know what to do. Finally, he stammered an apology, backed away. The fake professor gestured to the two minders, who walked him to the waiting car. He got in and left.

'It was clever,' Bryn said. 'You see, we all sort of knew what he looked like. We'd seen him on TV. And we knew he was going to be there. All the guy had to do was turn up and act like the famous professor. Nobody would guess he was a fake. That was what was so brilliant. He didn't have to fool us, we fooled ourselves. We saw exactly what we expected to see.'

'You didn't,' Jade murmured.

'I did to begin with,' Bryn reminded her. 'I was taken in too. Even when I was standing there talking to him. He fooled me. And I'd sat next to the real Laud in his car.

I'd got a lot closer to him than anyone else. It was only when he made that mistake about Ned that I realized he wasn't him.'

Jade said, 'Why go to all that trouble?'

'I don't know,' Bryn muttered, shaking his head. 'It seems odd.'

'Maybe he needed to be in two places at the same time,' Gil suggested. 'Perhaps that's what they do, famous people—hire a lookalike to impersonate them when they're too busy. Hey—I could do that. Get out of school for a few days.'

'Yeah, you're right. That must be it,' Bryn agreed. He was pretty sure it wasn't, but he didn't want to talk about it any more. Too many complications. He didn't want to talk about how the fake professor's eyes had blazed with hatred when he realized his disguise had been penetrated. How Bryn had felt paralysed with fear, locked into a steely blue gaze that glared out at him with a message that froze into his bones.

They reached his house. All at once, Bryn felt exhausted, depressed. He'd spent the whole day achieving nothing. 'Look, forget it,' he said wearily. 'It's probably not important, OK.' He turned to go in. 'I'll see you guys around, right?'

Gil watched Bryn go inside. 'You know what . . . ' he said slowly, 'I think there's more to this thing than he's telling us.'

Jade shrugged.

'You going my way?' Gil asked her.

'No.'

'See you then.'

Jade remained outside the house. She saw the light come on in Bryn's room. She pictured him there. Then flashes from the day started to form a montage in her mind: Bryn's expression as he leaned against the glass partition; Mr Neots talking animatedly, his bony fingers playing with a curl of red hair; two outriders dressed in black, their faces invisible under their black helmets. And she remembered something else too: a deep, dark sense of evil. She'd felt it twice that day. Once sitting in the canteen. And once again, as she stood and watched Bryn speaking to the fake Professor Laud.

Darya was upset. Her friend Kallie was suddenly acting very strangely. Almost as if she didn't like her any more. Darya couldn't understand it. Kallie was her best friend, wasn't she? Last week, they'd played together every recess. Shared their sweets and told each other private jokes. And when Darya's old friends wanted to join in, Kallie'd told them to piss off, which made Darya giggle with shock. She wasn't allowed to use bad words like 'piss off'. Kallie used plenty. She'd taught Darya most of them.

This week, however, Kallie was completely different. She didn't want to play. She didn't want to hang out with Darya any more. She'd suddenly gone stuck-up. When Darya had asked her why, Kallie'd replied: 'My dad has the ear of the President,' importantly.

'Eugh . . . that's disgusting!'

Kallie had rolled her eyes. 'You're *so* stupid,' she sneered. 'You don't understand anything.'

'I do so,' Darya pouted.

'Bet you don't even know who the President is.'

'Do too.'

'Oh yeah? Who is he then?' Kallie drawled, pulling her mouth into a mean shape and closing her eyes.

Darya had produced an opened chocolate bar from her pocket. It bore the familiar profile below the Globechoc logo. 'See,' she said. She held the gaily coloured wrapper towards Kallie.

Kallie viciously knocked the bar out of Darya's hand. 'Stupid little freck-face,' she cried.

Darya stared at her. Then looked down. Her chocolate bar had fallen into a muddy puddle. Darya's lower lip started quivering. A big tear rolled down her cheek. 'Look what you did,' she whispered. 'I can't eat that now.'

'Who cares?' Kallie tossed her curls, had started to walk off.

'I'm going to tell my brother,' Darya whimpered.

'Oh yeah?' Kallie turned, thrust her pointy face so close that Darya could see and almost count each individual red freckle. 'Go on then, crybaby. Tell, why don't you,' Kallie had hissed, 'only you better watch out. Cos why? *My* dad says *your* brother's in BIG trouble.'

Bryn was desperately worried. Something bad must have happened to Laud. But what? He couldn't stop thinking about what had occurred at the Open Day. It was like a bruise inside his head. He tried to direct his thoughts away, but they kept bumping against the question. Every time, Bryn flinched away from reaching any conclusion.

Finally, Bryn remembered the card. He decided he'd check out Laud's contact number. Just to confirm he was there. That he really existed and was all right. He typed in the code. Nothing happened. He tried again, got the same negative response. Over the next couple of days, Bryn tried repeatedly to establish contact. But there was no answer.

It seemed as if Professor Theo Laud had mysteriously dropped out of contact with the outside world.

Mu

J ade was also worried. There was something badly wrong with Bryn. He'd changed so much. Since the weekend of the Open Day, he'd become withdrawn, remote. He barely spoke, was wrapped in his private thoughts. He didn't want to spend time with her or with anybody. Whenever she thought about it, Jade swore softly to herself. How had it happened? It must've been something she said, something she did. Maybe she should have been more sympathetic, more involved. The big 'if only'—the story of her life!

Other people had noticed the change in Bryn too.

'Hey, garbo-head,' Jena greeted her mid-week as they were standing in line waiting for class, 'wassamatta with your boyfriend then?'

'Don't know,' Jade answered, then added, 'and he isn't my boyfriend.'

'Nah?' Jena's eyes widened in fake shock. 'D'ya meanter tell me you aren't going together?'

Heads turned to look at her. Embarrassed, Jade edged back along the line.

'Hey, I'm talking t'ya.'

Jade shrugged, turned her back, kept moving.

'So whatdid ya do? Scare him off?'

Jade pretended not to hear her. Selective deafness. It usually worked. Sure enough, after a couple more jibes, Jena lost interest. Muttering, she slid alongside one of her friends. Jade breathed a sigh of relief. She kept creeping back until she reached the end of the line. Then back a bit more. It was a technique she'd perfected over the years. As soon as the classroom door opened, everyone surged forwards, wanting to be the first in. She'd never understood why. Nobody ever noticed her slipping away. It worked every time.

Jade went to the girls' cloakroom, locking herself into a cubicle. Yawning, she sat down on the seat. Since the Open Day, she hadn't been sleeping well. She'd kept waking up suddenly in the middle of the night, imagining there were dark figures in her room. Then fear kept her awake for the rest of the night. Jade leaned her head against the cool white wall, closed her eyes. Everything was very quiet, very peaceful. Gradually, she felt her body relaxing, growing heavy. Next minute, she was fast asleep.

Kirrin had a very bad cold. He'd caught it walking home in the rain after the Open Day. Usually, he'd have had to go to school—his father didn't allow him time off. However, his dad had been in an unusually good mood, so for once Kirrin had been permitted to stay at home.

Kirrin liked being in the house without the poisonous atmosphere that hung around like a bad smell whenever his parents were in. He got up late, played on his computer, raided the fridge at regular intervals. Life was good. Even though he couldn't breathe without sneezing.

However, this was the third day he'd been at home and he was bored. He'd run out of things to do. There was nothing nice to eat—Kirrin usually did the shopping for the family. His dad didn't care, his mum couldn't cope. He wandered aimlessly through the house until eventually his steps led him to his father's study. He stood outside the door and listened. The house was so quiet you could have heard a fly cough; both his parents were at work. But Kirrin still felt a shiver of fear go through him as he pushed open the door.

Kirrin stood on the threshold of his father's sanctum. He'd never been in this room. Only Kallie was allowed to come and go freely. His mother had restricted access—she just came in to clean. He looked around. The walls were painted pale blue, making the room feel cool, remote. It was bare of pictures, ornaments, but scrupulously tidy. Folders, school textbooks were piled neatly on the wooden shelves. The pens on the desk were lined up in a row, soldiers on parade. Feeling like a criminal but unable to resist, Kirrin tiptoed across the floor. The temperature inside the room was quite cold, even though it was the height of summer outside. He slid into the swivel chair, sat listening. Silence. The only sounds to be heard were the wheeze of his breathing and the thump of his terrified heart.

Kirrin opened one of the desk drawers. It was full of disks, labelled in his father's small spidery writing. They all looked school related but eventually he found one labelled 'personal'. Kirrin lifted it out. Then, amazed at his own daring, he loaded it into his father's computer and scanned the menu. He saw a file labelled 'Surveillance Reports'. He clicked on it. A long list of names flashed on to the screen. Many of them were people Kirrin recognized, though thinking about it, he realized he'd not seen them recently. One name he recalled as belonging to a boy in the year above him. Kirrin thought he'd recently left. What on earth was going on?

Then a name suddenly leapt out at him. It was the name of somebody he very much admired. Somebody he desperately wanted to be like. Kirrin clicked on the name. Words appeared on the screen. His fear temporarily forgotten, he began reading.

Jade was startled awake. A gang of girls burst noisily into the cloakroom. She glanced at her watch, groaned. She had slept for a whole hour. Groggily, Jade levered herself upright, rubbing her eyes, flexing stiff shoulders. Meanwhile, the group got on with its activities. From behind the locked door, she could picture them clearly. Fixing their hair, applying make-up, making their tribal statement. Jade did not recognize any of the voices but the conversation was the usual girl-stuff—clothes, boys. Boring, boring, Jade thought, stifling a yawn.

More girls piled in. Now Jade recognized Jena's loud, strident tone. 'Yeah, so, like I said, Neots is finally going,' she announced.

Jade sat up even straighter, straining her ears to hear what was being said.

'You sure?' somebody asked.

'Hey listen, would I mistake on this? You know how much I hate the stob.'

'Wow! When?'

'Soon. Maybe coupla weeks.'

'Juice! Where's the stob going?'

'Heard it was the big city. Goingta some posh job with the government.'

'You sure?'

'Listen, my brother's in the same class as his girlbrat. Says she's been shooting the word all week. Good riddance I say,' Jena flounced.

'Aw, Jenz, you not going to get him a goodbye card then?' someone remarked to the sound of laughter.

'Yeah, right,' Jena sneered. 'Like mig I am. A big, exploding in yer face, frakk off and get lost card.'

There was more laughter. Then Jena started talking about boys and clothes. Jade sat frozen silent in the tiny cubicle. She waited until the last girl had gone before she came out, stretching her cramped legs. This was good news. The best. Worth celebrating. Jade decided to treat

herself to a nice lunch in the canteen. She ran her fingers
through her hair to tidy it and hurried out.

Bryn was playing Quantum Racer with Ned. Not
unusual, it was his favourite game. What was unusual
was that he was losing. The strange computer was much
faster. It could move through all six dimensions
simultaneously. Bryn didn't stand a chance. To rub salt
into his wounds, Ned had programmed its cybercrowd to
chant abuse at him every time it won. Bryn was refusing
to let it get to him. He tried to block Ned's lobster. Ned
launched a spacenet, entangled his blastcruiser and
moved into reverse hyperspeed. The crowd chanted:
'Loser, loser!!'

'OK. I give up. You win.'

'I am so sorry you appear to be having problems,' the
metallic voice said smugly. It didn't sound sorry at all.

'Yeah, right.'

'Would you like to play again?' the computer enquired
hopefully.

'No way.'

'As you wish.' Even though he knew it wasn't
technically possible, Bryn was sure the small black box
was smirking at him.

Bryn closed Ned's lid. Ned immediately split itself into
Ned and Little Ned and went on playing the game. Faint
sounds of cheering and abuse filtered out every now and
then. Bryn opened his books, tried to study. He'd fallen
back with his school work. Teachers were beginning to
threaten. Neots for one—Darya had told him what Kallie'd
said to her. Bryn had taken Darya's warning on board. He
knew Neots could make things very unpleasant if he
chose. Which he frequently did. He often reduced students
to tears with his sarky comments. Only Jena and Jade

appeared impervious. Jena because she didn't give a stuff for anyone. And Jade lived in a world of her own most of the time. Lucky them, he thought enviously. They didn't have half his problems.

Bryn skimmed through a chapter of his history textbook, then realized he hadn't taken in a word. He closed the book, sighed. He couldn't concentrate. His mind kept wandering even though there were very few places it could go. He glanced at his watch. Saw the text message icon was flashing. He pressed the receiving button. There was a brief message from Gil: *Catch the news*, it said.

Downstairs in the lounge, Darya was sitting in front of the TV. She had a big bag of corn chips on the sofa next to her. 'And I'm not going to invite her to my party,' she said indignantly as Bryn came in.

'Mmm-hmmm . . . ' Bryn was used to Darya continuing conversations that had happened ages ago. He slid next to her, grabbed a handful of chips and picked up the TV remote. He flicked it to the news channel. 'Just got to check something, Da,' he said. 'You can have your programmes back in a minute.'

He focused his attention on the screen. He watched a report on trade. Some nature stuff. New and better medical treatment. So? What did Gil mean? He was about to flick back to Darya's channel.

And then.

(Close-up of announcer's face)

'The death has been announced of a senior government minister,' (bland voice-over). *'Professor Theodore Laud, 55, who worked as senior scientific adviser to the President, was found slumped at the wheel of his car in the early hours of the morning.'*
(Cut to exterior of car)

'It is thought that Professor Laud, who had a history of heart trouble, suffered a massive coronary. Doctors who examined the body stated that death was probably instantaneous.'

(Microsecond pause)

'And now for the latest weather picture over to Sannie in our weather studio . . . '

Bryn flicked the TV back to the kids' channel. He sat staring at the screen, seeing nothing. His father was dead. Laud was dead. Who would be next?

Nu

The President sat at his desk. It was a very small desk, given who he was on a global scale. That was deliberate. If you had a big desk, people came in and dumped papers on it. He didn't want that happening. It upset his aesthetic sensibilities. So his officials had big desks. It made them feel important and kept them busy.

The President glanced around his office. It was a very small office for somebody whose face was universally recognized. That was how he liked it. If you had a big office, people came in and held meetings in it. He didn't like meetings. In the past, he'd attended far too many. They'd all been a waste of time. So his officials had big offices with panoramic views, comfortable chairs, and low tables. They were probably having a meeting in one of them right now, he thought. Talking. Wasting their time. Although not *all* of them, he reminded himself. Today, one face would be missing. One voice unheard. Ah well.

The President picked up a beautiful seashell that lay on his desk. He turned it over, marvelling at the way the colours changed from rose-pink to palest creamy-white. He held it to his ear, listening to the waves lapping against some faraway shore. Here was reality, he thought. The endless, ageless sound of the sea. He would have a new hologram made for his office. A tropical beach. Blue sea, white sand, seagulls calling. Yes. He drew a pad towards him, scribbled a note.

The President sighed gently. Professor Theodore Laud, he thought. A good man, as good men went. And as good men went, he had gone. Still, no person, no problem. Another man called Joseph Stalin had written that. A man from the past. Not, maybe, a good man, but a great man. You learned so much from studying great men. How to deal with people who upset you. How to keep everybody so busy that they had no time to interfere. No time to think. That was how you organized it. That was how you remained at the hub of things. The President liked that word. He wrote it down. Hub. Then he sat back in his chair and contemplated it, still holding the big shell up to his ear.

Bryn didn't believe it. It was all too convenient, too much of a coincidence. Whatever the official line, Laud's death was not natural. It had been planned, just like the 'tragic and unforeseen accident' of his father's death. Laud must have been getting close, Bryn thought. Too close. So they'd got rid of him. Just like his father. Because that was what they did with people who stood in their way. They got rid of them. Swiftly and ruthlessly.

Bryn fought hard against the feeling of rising panic. He knew the deaths weren't going to stop with Laud. No way. This was clearly too big, too important. One by one, all Laud's contacts would be traced and eliminated. Everybody who knew about the secret research. And of course, it wouldn't take them long to link Laud to his dad. Especially if the message was still on Laud's computer. And then Bryn thought about the things he'd let slip to the fake professor and realized he'd given them a link from both Laud and his dad to himself. And then? his brain screamed. *And then . . . ?*

It was just so typical of his father to wait until halfway through dinner before announcing anything important. It

92

was as if he deliberately wanted to spoil his family's enjoyment of their pudding. That was what Kirrin felt. He'd just picked up his spoon and was about to dig into a slice of chocolate gateau when his father broke the news.

'I shall be leaving my teaching post in the near future,' he said.

Silence. Kirrin and his mum exchanged puzzled glances. Kallie smirked.

'I have been offered a more senior position with a salary commensurate with my abilities,' Mr Neots went on pompously.

Why did he always have to use long words, Kirrin thought wearily. Couldn't he just say: I've got a better job with more money.

'When . . . is this . . . going to happen?' his mother asked hesitantly. She kept her face down, didn't make any eye contact.

'Soon. Very soon. My new role is one of senior adviser to a very high-up government official. I will, of course, have to move to the city.'

'Aw, Daddy!' Kallie yelped. 'You never said that.'

So she knew about it already, Kirrin thought. Slimy little toad.

'It will only be for a short time, my precious.' Mr Neots smiled.

'And then will we move to the city too?' Kallie asked.

'We shall see.'

'I want to move to the city,' Kallie pouted. 'I haven't got any friends. I hate it here.'

That's because you're such a poisonous creep, Kirrin thought. He glared across the table. Kallie intercepted his look, stuck out her disgusting chocolate-covered tongue.

Mr Neots pushed his plate away, rose from the table. 'I shall be working in my study for the rest of the evening,' he said coldly to his wife. 'There is a lot to do. I do not therefore expect to be disturbed.' He smiled at Kallie, then his fish-eyes swivelled round to rest upon Kirrin. Kirrin felt himself going scarlet. Sometimes, although he knew it was impossible, he was sure his father could tell exactly what he was thinking.

Right now, Kirrin especially didn't want him seeing anything. He was feeling guiltily terrified. He had copied one of his father's computer files. Tomorrow, when he returned to school, he intended to show it to Bryn. He badly wanted Bryn to be pleased with him, although he wasn't quite sure how he'd react to what he was about to discover. He hoped Bryn would get really angry and shout and swear at his father. That'd be good to watch.

Mr Neots curled his lip and glowered at his son. Then he turned on his heel and stalked out of the room. Watching him, Kirrin slipped into fantasy mode . . . maybe, he thought to himself, Bryn would be so cross with what he read that he'd pull out a knife and plunge it into his father's heart. Then he'd turn and smile at Kirrin. 'Mates?' he'd say. And Kirrin would nod agreement. They could always dispose of the body in one of the big wheelie-bins round the back of the canteen, he thought gleefully. Nobody would ever find out. Shovel it in with all the pigslop leftovers.

Kirrin went up to his room. So his father was moving to the city. Soon. Suddenly, the full implications hit him. No more rows, no more beatings. No more cruel words. Joy flooded Kirrin's soul. For the first time for ages, he felt truly happy. He unwrapped the bar of chocolate he'd been saving for later on. He had to celebrate the glorious news. He loaded his favourite game on to his Gamescom and deliberately turned his music up loud. He knew it annoyed his father. His study was directly below. But Kirrin no longer cared.

* * *

Mr Neots closed his study door. He thought about his family. How stupid they were, how useless. Except for Kallie, of course. She was the only worthwhile one. Kirrin he dismissed with a derisive snort. Obese loafer. No backbone, no ability. How many times had he asked him to perform some easy, menial task—like befriending the boy Bryn—only to discover that he was incapable of carrying it out. Procrastinating idler. He would be glad to be shot of him.

As for his wife. There must have been something there when he married her—apart from her money, of course. But what it was he couldn't now recall. There was nothing left now. Over the years she had dwindled into an inebriated nonentity. He had long ago stopped taking her with him when he attended formal functions. She was an embarrassment. He was not taking her with him now either. She would drag him down. Back to the drudgery of teaching pimply adolescents. Mr Neots shuddered. He would take Kallie instead. He'd easily find somebody to look after her whilst he worked. The other two could remain in this insignificant backwater and rot. Good riddance, he thought.

Mr Neots opened his briefcase. He had work to do. Important government work. He checked his e-mails and was soon so concentratedly absorbed in his tasks that he didn't even notice the thump-thump of Kirrin's music overhead.

Xi

'You're having me on, mate,' Gil said.

'No.'

'Ah, come on. It's a joke isn't it?'

'Look, that Open Day—I bet he was already dead. That's why they used a lookalike. Only they'd reckoned without me. They didn't know I'd met Laud. Once they realized I'd seen through their fake guy, they had to get rid of him. So they came up with the heart-attack thing. If I hadn't been there, they'd have kept the guy on. He'd have been Laud. Nobody'd have ever known.'

'And you're telling me this fake guy might be part of some gang that killed your father?' Gil was still sceptical.

'I believe it.' Jade spoke quietly from the corner of the room.

Gil rolled his eyes, lowered his voice. 'Sorry. She wanted to come.'

'No, you did right,' Bryn murmured. He looked at Jade. 'Do you? Why?'

'He was evil.' Jade stared straight ahead. 'I felt it. Like Neots. The same feeling.'

Gil shook his head slowly and sadly from side to side. Bryn ignored him. 'What do you mean—evil?' he asked her curiously.

Jade focused inward, eyes wide and concentrated. 'It's like a black river. It pours out of them,' she said slowly. 'You want to step out of its way but it follows you, tries to suck you in.'

There was a long silence.

'And you saw this black river?' Bryn asked at last. Jade nodded.

'Aw, puh-lease,' Gil exclaimed, 'this is the twenty-second century. Logic-out, will you both. Black rivers? It's just not rational.'

Jade shrugged, withdrew into her corner. 'Please yourself,' she muttered. If only Gil weren't here, she thought. She wanted to tell Bryn about the other things. The things she saw that nobody else did. She wanted to tell him what she was seeing now. A pattern was emerging, Jade thought. Reality and virtuality approaching each other. Gil's scepticism was preventing them coming together.

There was another awkward pause.

'OK, let's get back on track here,' Gil said finally, glaring at Jade. 'Why should the prof. and your dad be killed by a gang?'

Bryn sighed. 'I don't know—it's something to do with some secret research the company's doing. But even if I did know, I wouldn't tell you. Don't you see—the more you know, the more you're in danger too.'

Gil looked at him disbelievingly. 'So go to the police. I would.'

'I can't do that either; I haven't any proof.'

Gil struggled to understand. 'But even if you're right about the prof., they're hardly going to do anything to you. You only met him once, didn't you? Think about it, mate. You're not . . . well . . . important enough, are you?'

Bryn looked away. He so wanted Gil to be right.

'I'm right, aren't I?' Gil asserted. Bryn nodded. Gil shot a quick glance of triumph at Jade. 'Don't you agree?'

Jade said nothing. What was there to say, she thought. Gil wouldn't believe her. So she didn't tell them that it wasn't only evil she could see. She could see fear too. Fear was always cold and grey-white. And right now, it was streaming off Bryn like dry ice.

Kirrin had had the worst day. The news about his father had spread like wildfire. This meant from the moment he got to school, Kirrin found himself the centre of attention. Everyone wanted to seek him out. People kept coming up to him, telling him how much they hated his father. How they couldn't wait for him to leave. Briefly, Kirrin tasted the dizzy heights of universal popularity. But for the wrong reason. It was so not fair.

Then, as the day dragged on, the focus had shifted. Kirrin started getting hate messages on his computer. He was tripped up in the corridor. Salt was poured on his lunch. They couldn't get to his dad, so they hit on him— the next best thing. Revenge by proxy. It was so out of order. The one person he could have turned to, who might have helped him, wasn't there.

Kirrin had looked for Bryn all day. Finally, when he'd plucked up enough courage to ask a boy in Bryn's class where he was, he'd been told rudely to 'eat dirt, fat drelb'.

Kirrin trudged miserably homewards, under a sky doom-stacked with black rainclouds. His mind was preoccupied with thoughts of revenge. Revenge upon the people who'd mocked him, spoilt his food, ruined his day. Revenge upon the father who would have preferred him unborn. Kirrin's soul chafed inwardly. Rain fell in heavy leadlike drops upon his unprotected head. He didn't want to go home, couldn't face it. But he was getting soaked. Then he remembered: he was just a few streets away from where Bryn lived. He thought he also remembered the number of Bryn's house. He'd looked it up a while ago, when his father had ordered him to make friends. Kirrin made a decision: he'd go round to Bryn's now, he thought. He'd show him the file he'd copied from his dad. It would be revenge. Of a sort.

'He's right,' Bryn said.

'If you say so,' Jade responded. She stared at him, unblinking, her face expressionless. It was a technique she'd perfected over the years. Usually, it made people shut up and go away. In Bryn's case, she rather hoped it might have the opposite effect. Jade was glad Gil had left to do some work. Bryn wasn't going to open up while he was there. Too much to lose. Boys didn't share fears and feelings. She'd noticed that. Once, she'd honestly believed it was because they didn't have any. She knew different now.

Bryn stopped pacing the room, slid into his chair. Jade remained still and silent. What was she thinking? Bryn wondered. She gave so little away. Jade was unlike any girl he'd met. She was completely different to Jena. If Jena'd been here, she'd have said: 'Hey, quit stressin'. C'mon out an' party.' That was Jena's solution to all problems. Not this one, though. Bryn felt as if all the parties in the world couldn't drive away this feeling of mounting fear.

Jade remained quiet, waiting, willing Bryn to talk.

'I think it's all connected,' Bryn said at last. 'My father and Laud. And this machine.' He indicated Ned. 'I know it's about the secret research they're doing,' he went on. 'I don't understand what it's for or why it's so important that people have to be killed. My father found out about it— he used Ned to break into the computer system at Globechem. And he died. Laud was trying to find out what was going on too. That's why he wanted to borrow Ned.

And he's dead as well. So now there's just Ned left. Ned—and me.'

Jade listened. Her gaze never left his face.

'And I know it's stupid,' Bryn continued, 'I know Gil's right, but I can't stop thinking that one day . . . soon . . . they'll come looking for us.' His eyes flicked away from her. 'Bet you agree with Gil—crazy, eh?'

Jade shook her head. Bryn wasn't crazy, she thought. She heard horses galloping in the empty air, felt the world was coming to an end. She woke in the night to see dark shadows moving in corners. Crazy was just a word for a shift in perspective. A journey to the far side of reality.

Suddenly there was a loud knocking on the front door.

Kirrin was having last-minute doubts. Suppose Bryn wasn't in? If he was in, suppose he didn't want to see him? Nobody else did. Suppose instead of being angry with his father, Bryn got angry with him? Kirrin didn't think he could take much more. He knocked on the door again, his hand automatically dipping into his pocket for some comfort sweets.

There was a pattering of feet. A small girl's voice asked: 'Who's that?'

'Kirrin Neots. Is Bryn there?'

There was a long pause. Kirrin was just about to knock again when the little girl asked suspiciously, 'Are you Kallie's big brother?'

'Yeah.'

'I hate her,' the little girl on the other side of the door announced.

'So do I,' Kirrin agreed automatically.

The door was instantly opened. 'He's upstairs,' Darya said pointing.

Kirrin mounted the stairs. Which room was Bryn's, he

100

wondered. A door suddenly opened. Bryn shot out onto the landing. Behind him was the strange girl. To Kirrin's surprise, they both looked white-faced, wide-eyed, and terrified. Then Bryn recognized him. His expression changed, relaxed.

'Oh, it's only you,' he said, in a relieved tone.

Kirrin felt a lump in his throat. It was the nicest thing anybody'd said to him all day.

Darya sat watching TV. She was trying not to care about Kallie. She had lots of other friends, she reminded herself. Sad things happened to everybody. She'd still have a lovely birthday party even if Kallie wasn't coming. Maybe she could ask Bryn's girlfriend to come instead. She seemed nice. Nicer than Darya had thought when she'd first met her. And Kallie didn't like her at all, Darya reminded herself. So she must be OK.

She heard footsteps overhead. The door to Bryn's room opened. Then Bryn yelled: 'Darya! Get up here now!'

Bryn, Kirrin, and Jade were gathered round Bryn's computer. They were peering at some writing on the screen. As Darya came in, they all turned and looked at her. Bryn's face was stern, serious. The other two looked worried. Darya's lower lip started to quiver.

'Da,' Bryn said. 'Have you taken anything from my room recently?'

'No,' Darya shook her head, 'I haven't.'

'Think, Da. Something like a plastic card with gold dots. Do you remember it?'

'No.'

'Small card, about this big.' Bryn's hands made a shape in the air.

'No,' Darya said stubbornly, 'I haven't seen anything like that.'

Bryn frowned. Clearly he didn't believe her. A fat tear rolled down Darya's cheek. She hated it when she and Bryn fell out. Especially when it wasn't her fault.

Bryn turned back to the others. 'I don't know,' he said, speaking softly, 'I hate to think she's lying. She must have taken it, though. Nobody else has been in here.'

Darya thought hard. 'Yes they have!' she cried. She shot Kirrin a quick glance. 'Kallie could've taken it. We played hide and seek here one day. I remember one time, she took ages coming to find me. She could've come in your room easily. I bet she did and she took it then.'

Kirrin bit his lip. 'She's probably right, you know,' he said. 'It's just the sort of thing my sister'd do. She's always poking her nose into places. She's taken my stuff and lied about it before. And that would explain how my father got hold of it.'

'See!' Darya said triumphantly. 'I told you it wasn't me.'

Bryn came over, put an arm round Darya's small indignant shoulders. 'Sorry, Da,' he said, 'I should have believed you, shouldn't I.'

'What was it she took?' Darya asked.

'Nothing,' Bryn lied, 'it wasn't important. Don't worry about it.'

'Here,' Kirrin said, 'would you like some of my sweets?'

Slightly mollified, Darya helped herself to a handful of candies. 'Can I stay and play with you?' she asked hopefully.

'Later, Da,' Bryn said. 'We have to do some boring school stuff now.' He placed his hand on her back and propelled her gently out of the room. He shut the door.

Darya stood on the landing listening, but there was no sound from inside Bryn's room. She frowned. What was all that about? Why had Bryn got so cross one minute and then said it didn't matter the next? It was perplexing. Still, she'd got Kallie into trouble and been given a big handful of sweets. So maybe, on reflection, everything had turned out all right. Satisfied, Darya trotted downstairs again. Justice had been done.

'I'm sorry,' Kirrin mumbled into the silence. 'I thought you should know . . . ' the words tailed off.

'No, mate, you did right,' Bryn said, 'thanks.' He continued peering distractedly at the screen.

Reluctantly, Kirrin picked up his bag. 'Well, I suppose I'd better go.' He paused, waiting for Bryn to suggest otherwise. Bryn didn't.

'OK then. Well, see you.' Kirrin headed for the door.

'Yeah, see you.' Neither Bryn nor the weird girl looked round.

At least it had stopped raining, Kirrin thought as he made his way downstairs. And he had done the right thing showing Bryn the file. Hadn't he?

'I don't get how this happened.' Bryn shook his head in disbelief. He gestured at the screen. 'Where did he get all this stuff about my dad?' His voice became thick with anger. 'It's all a pack of lies. He wasn't a cyber-terrorist— he was just trying to find out things. What is all this crap?' He banged his fist into the screen. 'I'm going to kill him! The lying bastard!'

Jade spoke into his pain. 'Maybe you need to think about yourself.'

'What do you mean?'

'Hatred can make you stronger or weaker,' Jade said, getting up. 'You have to choose.'

Bryn glanced at her questioningly.

Jade went over to the window. 'If it makes you weaker,' she said, 'you become like them. Then they've won. If you want to survive, you have to be strong.'

Bryn looked at her. Jade was speaking with confidence and power. He'd not heard her talk like this before. She spoke as if she had insight, experience. All at once, he saw her in a new and different light. He was impressed.

'Anyway,' Jade continued, staring out at the darkening summer sky. 'Neots isn't your problem. It's the others. The ones pulling his strings. I bet they're the same ones who killed your father. And Professor Laud too.' Jade turned from the window, looked directly at Bryn.

'Find their weak spot,' she said. 'Then you can begin to fight back.'

Omicron

Mr Neots smiled in a reptilian manner. A ripple of fear ran round the room. He'd been in a good mood for days. It was scaring the heck out of everybody. Tucked behind Jade, Bryn fixed his eyes on the middle of Neots's forehead, avoiding looking into his flat fishlike grey eyes.

This was his strategy. His coping mechanism.

Bryn imagined his gaze to be a white-hot laserbeam. It was burning a hole in Neots's skull. Smoke issued from his skin, which fizzled, turned black. Then the hole appeared, spread, grew wider. Now pale brain curds were oozing out, dripping down his face. The face was melting, the body was melting. Neots was dripping onto the floor like a wax candle. It was like playing Skullwars. And winning every time. It made him strong. It helped him stay in control. He wasn't absolutely sure what Jade would think but, hey, it worked for him.

Mr Neots eye-contacted all the students, mentally noting those who did not respond. The loudmouthed idler in the first row was cleaning under her nails, he observed. The boy Bryn was grinning in an inane fashion, the mad girl was staring at the wall. Cretinous loafers, he thought. He pitied his successor. He'd have his work cut out for him.

'Today,' Mr Neots announced, 'we will continue our study of the twenty-first century.'

Heads bent submissively over workstations.

'We shall consider the development of economic unity . . . ' Mr Neots paused, glared down at Jena, who had made no effort to activate her workscreen. 'Those of us who think they have more important things to do have not forgotten that there is a three hour exam next week, have they?' he enquired smoothly. Jena glanced up, scowled, switched on her workstation.

Mr Neots continued: 'After the great cybercrash of 2052, it was decided that the concept of nationalistic and internationalistic commerce had failed. The idea of separate companies all over the globe producing differing goods and services was no longer workable. There were not enough controls in place. Too many opportunities for unscrupulous self-motivated individuals or institutions to break the rules. Thus out of chaos rose the company that became known as Globetraid . . . '

Bryn's fingers typed. His mind roamed free. *Find their weak spot. Then you can begin to fight back.* It hadn't made sense at the time. Now he understood. Now he had a plan, a purpose. Bryn smiled wryly. And in a way, he thought, he actually owed it to Neots. Neots had given him the idea. Thrown him the concept by calling his father a cyber-terrorist. The distance from concept to reality was the click of a computer key.

Bryn had become a cyber-terrorist.

It had been relatively easy to do. Over the weekend, he and Ned had hacked into the school's computer network and with Ned's help, Bryn had set up a bogus subnetwork. By creating a fake address, covering his tracks, he hoped nobody would find him. He'd installed a firewall to stop anyone from getting in and to protect files he might want to download. Now Ned was trying to break into the Globechem system. Bryn hadn't yet decided what he was going to do when he got in. He might crash the mainframe or just look around. That decision was on hold. Until he'd discovered what was there.

106

' . . . the philosophy behind Globetraid is very simple,' Mr Neots droned on, 'unity and parity,' he paused, checking they were all writing this down. 'Unity and parity,' he repeated, 'the same products at the same prices wherever they are sold. Better quality. Fairer choice.'

He sounds like a politician, Bryn thought. A boring politician. Not like Laud. Laud didn't talk down to people, treat them as if they were ignorant, stupid. He glanced quickly around the room. Everybody was working. Heads down, hands moving. They never questioned. Never thought. Just absorbed uncritically. Like sponges.

Looking at them, Bryn realized how much he'd changed. Before his father's death, he'd taken everything for granted too. Lived in a small world of his own. Now, his perception of that world had changed. He had glimpsed the skull beneath the skin. Now he was afraid.

Mr Neots lectured on. It was his duty to instil truth into minds. And he would do so, right up to the final seconds of his last day. Mr Neots knew there would be no farewell party after school, no good luck card and jovial speeches. He was disliked by his colleagues nearly as much as by his students. He didn't care. They were a lacklustre bunch. Uninspiring dullards. Incapable of seeing beyond the textbook. Blinkered poltroons. He would not miss them.

There were so few individuals who deserved his respect, he thought sadly: his contact in the government secret service—the one Kallie called 'the man in the posh car'. One could admire his swift and ruthless efficiency. Anyone else? Yes. Neots's aquiline features softened. The President. Though respect was hardly the right word. Loyalty, devotion, worship—were better words, though they too fell short of his true feelings. And soon, he reminded himself, if everything went to plan, he might actually meet the great man, ruler of the universe, face to face.

Meanwhile, the President sat in his office contemplating an object. It was a small white card with a pattern of raised gold dots. The President knew what it was. Although he had not seen one for a very long time. He lifted it carefully, holding it close to his face. He looked at it, closed his eyes, opened them again.

The President considered the existence of objects. Did something exist only when it was there in front of your eyes? Or did it have a real existence. Maybe this card was merely the product of somebody's imagination, now invested with the appearance of reality.

The President contemplated the nature of perception. To see or not to see. That was the question. Sometimes the answer was to close one's eyes, deny that things were. He thought about things that did and did not exist. Africa. The Third World. Other similarly hopeless places. The President remembered the stick people. Always starving. You sent them food. Helped them get back on their feet. Then they fought each other, starved all over again. An endless cycle. It couldn't go on. So you put a stop to it. No more food, you said. No more stick people. That was after the time the harvests failed. There wasn't enough food to go round anyway. It's us or them, you said. Nobody said anything in reply. Hunger focuses the mind wonderfully.

And then?

The computer virus struck. Silently, lethally. It raced around the world at light speed. A global pandemic. Everything was wiped out. You had to recreate the world's infrastructure from scratch. It took a long, long time.

And afterwards, nobody remembered what had happened to the stick people.

As you intended.

And now?

Maybe there were still stick people out there, crawling in the thick orange dust, searching for food. Or maybe not. Perhaps there was only the vast horizon-touching desert, where the sun beat down and it hadn't rained for over a hundred years.

Ah well. One of the advantages of living far longer than anybody else was that you saw how fragile the future was. The Technological Revolution, the Eradication of Disease, the Elimination of World Hunger—so many big things had been predicted. And where were the predictors? Dead and forgotten, like their words. What changed history were tiny things.

The click of a computer key.

I am, he thought. Or do I merely think I am.

The President brought his mind to the reality of the present. The card. He picked it up, held it in the palm of his thin-veined hand. He sighed. Why must his equilibrium be constantly disturbed? The boy again, he thought. The one he'd dismissed as unimportant. But now it appeared that the boy had connections. Important connections. Something would have to be done, the President thought. He could not let someone as trivial as this boy interfere with his plans. Not now that he was so close to completion.

So . . . to do or not to do. That was now the question. Ah, decisions, decisions, the President thought. Always decisions. He sighed. Then flicked the card high in the air, so that the raised gold dots glittered in the light. Gold side up, he did nothing, gold side down, he took appropriate action.

The card landed on his desk. Gold side down.

* * *

'We've done it!' Bryn exclaimed.

Ned treated itself to a loud fanfare and a ripple of applause. They had been trying to break into Globechem. It had been hard, even though Bryn knew how the passwords were constructed and, in theory, Ned had got in before. But for a long time, Ned had failed to penetrate the tight security wall that now surrounded the system. And then, unbelievably, 'password accepted' had flashed on to the screen. They were in.

'How did you do that?' Bryn asked admiringly.

'I attached myself to an incoming message,' Ned informed him in a bored tone.

Bryn wasn't fooled. He knew Ned was enjoying itself. After all, this was what it had been designed to do.

'That's clever.'

'It's an old method.' Ned faked modesty.

'I'd never thought of doing it like that.'

'No . . . ' There was a whole world of meaning in Ned's voice. Bryn chose to ignore it.

'Do you want me to load a virus package?' Ned asked.

'Not yet. Just look around,' Bryn instructed. 'See if you can find anything. Files labelled classified. Stuff like that.'

'Roger. Wilco. Chocks away, squadron leader.'

Bryn groaned. Names and codes flashed across the screen to the accompaniment of stirring military music. Why did Ned have to make such a big deal about everything? Bryn looked at the little machine, shook his head sadly. What was it like!

Meanwhile Jade was shopping. Not for herself. She was buying a gift for Darya's birthday. Jade had never been to a kids' party. She was flattered Darya had invited her, though Bryn had warned her privately that it was going to be loud and chaotic and she was mad to say she'd come.

Jade browsed along the toystore shelves. Everything was so brightly coloured. So relentlessly in-your-face. So tacky. Was this the sort of stuff she used to play with? Jade thought back to her childhood. What had she enjoyed doing when she was small? Being outside, she remembered that. Playing in the garden. And? Jade screwed up her face in concentration. She used to grow things—flowers. Of course! Jade's face brightened. She turned her back on the lurid, garish toys, marched out of the shop. Forget this trash, she thought. She'd get Darya something good. Something lasting. She headed for the garden shop.

In the walkway, Jade ran into Kirrin. He was munching something large, greasy-looking, and pink-iced. For Kirrin, the line between snack and meal was blurred.

'Want some?' Kirrin offered.

Shuddering, Jade shook her head. How could anyone eat that stuff? she wondered. Just looking at it made her teeth edgy.

'I've got the latest Lasertramp,' Kirrin told her proudly through a mouthful of cake.

'Mm-hmm.'

'You might tell Bryn, when you see him next.'

Jade nodded. She wasn't sure she liked Kirrin. Admittedly her feelings had a lot to do with his father. And his food habits. As if reading her mind, Kirrin leaned forward and said in a low, sticky voice, 'You heard about my dad?'

'Yeah.'

'He's leaving end of next week.'

'Uh-huh.'

'We're not going with him.'

'No?' Jade started edging away. Kirrin smelt of cake, his face was shiny and hot.

'D'you like your father?' Kirrin asked abruptly.

111

'Huh?'

'I loathe mine.' Kirrin's voice was unexpectedly harsh. 'I loathe him every minute of every day and night.' He stared at Jade, daring her to be shocked. Then, when she made no reply, he turned and stomped off, his fat shoulders stiff with suppressed hatred.

Jade watched Kirrin go. She almost felt pity for him. If she had a father like Neots, she'd definitely feel spewed out. She went to the garden shop to buy her seeds. On the way, she thought about her own parents. She neither liked nor disliked them. They were just there. Though not very often nowadays. They kept the fridge full, paid her allowance, and let her get on with her life. It wasn't a bad deal. All things considered.

Jade wondered fleetingly about her birth father. Her only connection with him was the clinic number on her birth card. And the meagre details she'd picked up as she'd grown. Still, she decided, what did it matter who he was. He was never going to make contact after all this time. Probably dead by now. So, fine. Hey, no big deal. She was content with the way things were. Compared to Kirrin, she had it easy.

Pi

Kallie Neots was sulking. Everybody was going to Darya's party. Kallie couldn't believe Darya was so mean as to leave her out. And after she'd tried so hard to make up with her.

Mean mean Darya.

Kallie really wanted to go to the party. She had a brand new dress. It was special, a designer one, much more expensive than anybody else's. And she wanted to brag a bit more about her dad's new job. Instead, here she was, stuck at home on a bright sunny afternoon.

Nothing to do. Nobody to impress.

Kallie went in search of Kirrin. She pushed open his bedroom door. Kirrin was playing computer games.

'Frakk off,' he said, not even turning round.

Kallie stuck out her tongue.

'D'you hear me?' Kirrin said. 'This is my room. You're not allowed in here.'

Kallie stared at him. 'I can do what I like,' she said stubbornly, 'Daddy says so.'

'Yeah well,' Kirrin spun round. 'Daddy's not going to be here much longer, is he? So you better watch out.' He finished his game, re-boxed the disk and got up.

'Where you going?'

'Out.'

'Out where?'

'None of your business.'

'I'll tell.'

Kirrin shrugged. He pushed her out of his room, closed

113

the door behind him. 'Aren't you invited to Darya's party then?' he taunted. Kallie's expression hardened.

'Aw,' Kirrin teased. 'Poor little Kallie. Never mind, I'll get her to save you some cake.'

Kallie's mouth dropped open. *'You're* going to Darya's party?'

'Yeah.' Actually, Kirrin was only dropping off the game. He wasn't telling his sister that, though. 'Hey, shame about you,' he grinned maddeningly.

Kallie scowled. She tried blocking the landing, but Kirrin elbowed her roughly out of the way. She stuck out her foot, but Kirrin kicked it aside. 'Bad luck, loser,' he scoffed, 'enjoy yourself. All on your own.'

Kallie's eyes shot daggers at his retreating back. She waited till he'd left the house, then tried the handle of his door. No luck. Kirrin must've locked it. Frakk, frakk! Kallie went to her room, slammed the door. She spent a long time swearing and throwing her toys around. They'd better watch out, she thought darkly. Darya, Bryn, all of them. Most of all her fat pig-brother. She'd pay them all back. Just see if she didn't!

'Told you it'd be crazy,' Bryn shouted. The noise of thirteen kids running round the garden having fun was deafening. Jade smiled back bravely. She had two small girls attached to each hand. They were pulling in opposite directions. Her arms felt as if they were coming out of their sockets. 'It's OK,' she shouted back. 'I'm enjoying it, really.'

Bryn's mum came out of the house, beckoned him over. 'Can you round them up and bring them into the living room?' she asked.

'Is it teatime already?'

'Not yet. There's a man with a puppet show arrived. He's just setting up.'

'Huh?'

'He says Dad ordered it ages ago. As a special secret surprise for Da's birthday.' Bryn's mum looked a little flustered. 'I don't remember him telling me. Did he mention it to you?'

'No. But then he had a lot on his mind, didn't he.'

His mum's face cleared. 'Yes. Yes, you're right. It must have slipped his mind. Oh well—we'd better pretend it was our idea, hadn't we? Don't want to upset Darya on her birthday.' She indicated Jade. 'Maybe your friend might like to come and help me in the kitchen. There's a lot of food to get ready.'

'Sure.'

Bryn got the kids into the living room, seated them on the carpet in front of a brightly coloured yellow and red striped puppet theatre set up by the French windows. The kids wriggled and fidgeted. There was a buzz of excitement. Suddenly a dog puppet appeared and began twirling a string of pink sausages round its head. Everyone yelled with delight.

Bryn stood at the back watching the show. The puppeteer was very funny; Darya was really loving it. Good old Dad, he thought. Pity you can't be here to see Da enjoying herself. The plot seemed to be about the dog stealing sausages from a butcher. It involved lots of terrible jokes and fast chases. The kids joined in loudly. Finally, the dog was cornered. A new puppet appeared. It was dressed in black, had a thin, elderly face, deep socketed eyes. Bryn grinned. It was obvious who it was meant to represent. 'Hello, boys and girls,' the puppet said. 'Do you know who I am?'

'The President!' several voices called out in unison.

'That's right,' the puppet nodded. 'And what am I going to do?'

'Catch the dog.'

'Smack it.'

'Get the sausages.'

'You're quite right. I'm going to do all those things.'

The audience cheered. The President puppet pretended to smack the dog. The audience howled with laughter.

'That's the way to do it!' the dog shouted.

'Oh no it isn't,' the audience yelled back.

'Oh yes it is!'

'Oh no it isn't!'

'OH YES IT IS!' the President puppet said loudly. The laughter died. The puppet stared out into the audience. 'Hello, Bryn,' it said quietly. There was a gasp of amazement. Bryn froze.

'Yes, I know all about you, Bryn,' the puppet went on. 'Everything you do. I've been watching you very closely for a long time. Do you know what happens to naughty boys, Bryn?'

Silently, Bryn's lips formed the word 'No'.

'I'll tell you what happens.' The puppet reached down, picked up a gun. It pointed the gun straight at Bryn. 'This is what happens,' it said, pulling the trigger. There was an enormous bang. Bryn threw himself sideways. Everybody screamed. Then the space in front of the stage exploded into a shower of rainbow coloured balloons and streamers. Blue smoke filled the room. The kids jumped up, grabbing for balloons.

Bryn lay on the floor. Dimly, from far away, he heard someone call his name. He opened his eyes, looked up. Jade was standing in the doorway. 'Your mum says tea's ready,' she said. 'What are you doing down there?'

Bryn staggered dazedly to his feet. 'What?'

'Tea's ready,' Jade repeated. 'And she says would you ask the puppet-man if he'd like a drink.'

Bryn looked over the heads of happy, dancing, balloon waving children. The French windows were open, curtains moving gently in the summer breeze. The puppet theatre had gone.

Bryn paced restlessly. Jade sat on the bed, watching him. Through the half-open door filtered the sounds of the party beginning to wind down.

'He knew my name,' Bryn said incredulously. 'He said he knew all about me.'

'He might've been joking?'

'How could I have been so stupid! Dad would never have ordered a puppet show without telling us.' Bryn threw himself into his chair, dropped his head in his hands, groaned. 'This isn't happening. Tell me it isn't happening.'

Jade pleated the edge of the duvet cover. 'Who was he, do you think?'

'I don't know. He must have been somebody in the gang. Maybe the guy who killed Dad. Or the guy who impersonated Laud. Hey, maybe he really was the President.'

'I don't think so,' Jade said, considering. 'You're absolutely sure he wasn't . . . just joking around?'

'Am I laughing?' Bryn exclaimed. 'I thought he was going to shoot me. I've never felt so frightened in my life.'

'Maybe you should report him to the cops.'

'Oh yeah. Right. What'd I say? "Please, sir, this glove puppet was scaring me." Nice one. They'd laugh themselves silly. Anyway, I can't go to the police.'

'Why not?'

Bryn grimaced, averted his gaze. 'They don't like me.'

'How come?'

'See, when Dad died, I sort of flipped for a bit. I kept going down to the factory, asking questions, trying to find out what happened. I used to go down late at night too.

Just stood around, nothing major. But after a bit, they complained to the police, said I was "harassing employees". My mum got really upset. I can't cause her any more grief.'

'Right,' Jade nodded. 'So what are you going to do?'

There was a long silence. Finally Bryn spoke. 'I can't stay here,' he said dully. 'This was just a warning. They want me to know they know about me. They'll be back, for sure. And perhaps next time they might choose to do something to Da or Mum. I promised Dad I'd look after them.' Bryn looked at Jade. 'So maybe I need to find somewhere to hang out for a while. Just until they lose interest in me. Got any bright ideas?'

Jade thought hard. Then unexpectedly, she smiled. 'Yeah,' she said, 'you know what, actually I have.'

Kirrin arrived as the last guests were leaving. Jade had already gone. He waited on the doorstep until Bryn came out to see him.

'Oh, hi,' Bryn said, not making eye contact, 'umm . . . what's happening?'

Kirrin thought he looked unwell. 'I brought you this,' he said holding out a copy of Lasertramp. 'You said you wanted to borrow it sometime.'

'Oh. Right. Er, thanks.' Bryn took the box.

'You OK?' Kirrin asked hesitantly. Bryn seemed a bit distracted.

'Me? Fine.' Bryn seemed to pull himself together. 'Look, mate, thanks for this. OK if I keep it for a while? Only I'm going away.'

'Away? Where?'

'Uh . . . up north.' Bryn's voice sounded as if he was repeating a learned statement. His face was expressionless. 'I'm going to stay with some rellies.'

118

'When are you going?'

'Later tonight. Got some packing to do, then I'm off.'

'But what about school?' Kirrin asked.

'Jade'll sort it,' Bryn told him. 'Anyway, it's the last week of term, right. So we won't be doing much.'

Kirrin shifted from one foot to the other. He couldn't think of anything to say. 'So when will you be back?' he asked finally.

Bryn shrugged. 'Don't know. Whenever. You know what it's like.' He turned to go in.

'You can keep the game as long as you like,' Kirrin called out after him desperately.

'Thanks.'

The front door closed. Kirrin felt the finality of it. Another week of continued unpleasantness stretched ahead of him, he thought. And there would be no Bryn to turn to. Not for ages. Kirrin sighed sadly. His shoulders drooped; he felt bereft. His hand reached into a pocket for a consoling snack. He ate it, then slouched unhappily home.

Bryn returned to his room. Don't think about what's happening, he told himself. Just get on with what you have to do now. One step after another. He reminded himself he'd already taken the first step: laying a false trail.

Bryn flipped Ned's lid open. The small computer chuntered into life.

'You finished copying that file?' he asked.

'Affirmative. Mission accomplished,' Ned's voice saluted.

'Run it by me, can you.'

Ned went into display-with-appropriate-background-muzak mode. Bryn read through the data. It seemed to be a report written by an unnamed researcher at Globechem. Bryn understood most of it but there were a few words he'd never heard before.

'What are smallpox, anthrax, and plague?'

119

'Highly infectious diseases of the nineteenth and twentieth centuries,' Ned informed him in a bored voice. 'Generally fatal. All are officially extinct.'

'If they're extinct, why is somebody re-inventing them?'

Ned made its verbal equivalent of a shrug.

'Strange.' Bryn shook his head. He contemplated his next move.

'Do you wish to upload the daemon now?' Ned asked.

It was tempting. Bryn had learned that he could plant the virus code (Ned called it a daemon) in remote corners of the gigantic Globechem network. When he decided to activate it, the attack would look as if it came from within. Multiple sites would also make it harder to pin down and locate.

'Go on then.'

'What name shall I use?'

Bryn thought. 'Let's call it NEOTS, shall we?' he said grimly. He typed in the final instruction.

There was a nanosecond pause.

'File uploaded,' Ned said.

Later, when the house was quiet, Bryn crept downstairs carrying a heavily loaded rucksack. He left the letter telling his mum he'd taken a last minute place on a school trip, would be back soon. He stood in the hall for a while, breathing in the smell of the house, listening to the familiar sounds. He suddenly realized how much he was going to miss his home, his family. For a moment Bryn hovered on the brink of leaving. Then he closed the front door silently and stepped out into the late blue summer evening.

Rho

Gil was mystified. Most lunchbreaks, he and Bryn
got together to play virtual chess. It was a regular
meet. If one of them was ill, they played using
their mobiles. But today, Bryn failed to show. He paged
him at home, but he didn't reply. Gil was puzzled: Bryn
wasn't in school, he wasn't at home. Where was he?

Restlessly, Gil wandered round the computer centre.
He didn't want to face the idea that Bryn might have been
right and was even now being interrogated by government
secret agents. Gil hadn't believed it then. He wouldn't let
himself believe it now. There was a logical explanation for
his friend's unaccountable absence. Like there was always
a logical explanation for everything that happened.

On his second tour, he came across Kirrin sitting on
his own, being ignored. Kirrin glanced up hopefully as Gil
passed.

'You looking for Bryn?' he asked.

Gil paused, stared down. 'Why? You know where he
is?'

'Yeah. He told me he was visiting family. Up north, he
said.'

'Huh?'

Kirrin repeated the information. Gil's expression passed
from baffled incomprehension to utter disbelief. 'He hasn't
got any family up north,' he said bluntly.

'Perhaps he didn't tell you about them,' Kirrin said,
instantly regretting the remark.

Gil's face darkened with anger. 'Listen, *mate*,' he

121

exclaimed loudly. 'I've known Bryn since we were kids, right. I know all his family. So I'm telling you now that it isn't true, OK?'

'Right,' Kirrin mumbled, trying to shrink down into his chair. He was aware of the intense interest their conversation was generating. All over the room, heads were going up like surfacing gophers.

Gil glared at him. 'You want to check your facts,' he said.

'Right,' Kirrin repeated, trying to become part of the furniture.

Gil strode off. Kirrin watched him. Then, with a huge sigh he turned back to the screen. The hate messages were still coming through.

Gil decided to find Darya. He took a shortcut through the science block, crossing the playground to the junior area. Darya was playing with a group of friends. They were all running in a circle, screaming. Gil called her name. Darya broke free and ran across.

'Hi, Gil, did you hear about my party?'

Gil shook his head.

'It was the best time ever,' Darya cried. 'There was this puppetman and he pretended to shoot us.'

'Mmm.' Gil had never mastered the art of speaking to young children. 'Darya, where's Bryn?'

'He's on the field trip.'

'What field trip?'

'The field trip,' Darya said again. 'You know. There was a spare place came up suddenly so he decided to go.'

'Ah,' Gil nodded, catching on, 'the field trip.'

'Mum's not too pleased. She has to pay a sitter. I'm going to ask Jade.'

'Jade's not on this . . . field trip?'

'No, silly, or she couldn't sit for me.'

It was the only logical statement in an increasingly illogical world, Gil thought despairingly.

'He'll be back soon,' Darya shouted across the playground.

Gil hurried away shaking his head. There was no field trip. Just like there was no family. Now there was no Bryn. Three negatives, Gil thought. All of which added up to nothing positive.

Jade stopped off at the Globemart Foodstore. She bought two pizzas, two large bottles of water, and a couple of bananas. She stood in line waiting to pay with her babysitting money. As usual, she was in a world of her own. She balanced the basket on her hip, stared straight ahead, deep in thought. She didn't notice Kirrin standing in the next line. Kirrin was stocking up on cake and sweets, his favourite comfort foods. He was still feeling upset.

Kirrin glanced across, then down into Jade's basket. He knew Jade had no brothers or sisters. So why was she buying two of everything, he thought to himself? She had no friends either. Only Bryn, he reminded himself. *Who was visiting rellies that didn't exist*—Gil's startling revelation had really shocked Kirrin. He had not got Bryn down as a liar. And now here was Bryn's girlfriend, buying two pizzas. Kirrin wasn't stupid, in spite of his father's opinion. He could add up. He could make connections. Kirrin paid for his food and left the store. All at once, he felt better. He was glad he'd seen Jade. Things were beginning to fall into place.

Mr Neots was annoyed. His carefully laid plans had been disrupted. The boy Bryn, a pupil he greatly mistrusted, was missing. Frankly, Mr Neots couldn't care less about this. Personally, he wouldn't lose sleep if he never saw Bryn again. But others cared. He had just received a curt message from his contact. He was to locate the boy. It was important. Mr Neots fumed inwardly. As if it was his job to chase around after some errant teenage truant! He was no obsequious lackey, he thought angrily. He was not at everyone's beck and call. He was moving on. He was heading for a greater destiny, a higher calling.

Slamming his study door, Mr Neots strode to the foot of the stairs, calling loudly for Kallie and Kirrin. Kallie, red curls flying, ran lightly down to her father. She looked up at him expectantly. Kirrin lurked at the top of the stairs, his face pale, eyes remote and watchful.

'Do either of you know the whereabouts of young Bryn?' Mr Neots asked, his voice deceptively casual.

'He's on a field trip, Daddy,' Kallie piped.

Pure habit made Kirrin disagree automatically. 'Don't be stupid, he's . . . ' he began. Then realizing what he'd done he stopped, closed his mouth tight. His father and Kallie stared up at him.

'Yes . . . ?' Mr Neots questioned.

'Don't know.' Kirrin shook his head innocently. 'Sorry.' He refused to meet their joint gaze. 'Got to go. Things to do,' he muttered, backing into his room. Mr Neots looked thoughtfully at the space where Kirrin had just been. His eyes narrowed. 'I think your brother knows where Bryn is,' he murmured.

'He's fibbing, isn't he, Daddy?' Kallie said self-righteously.

'Indeed, precious.'

'Are you going to punish him?'

Mr Neots stroked his chin with his thumb and forefinger. 'Not yet,' he said slowly. He smiled down at Kallie. 'But I might. If I had proof.' He looked Kallie straight in the eye. There was a brief silence. Then Kallie nodded slyly. She understood perfectly.

Bryn finished the last succulent slice of cold day-old pizza. He licked his fingers. This was definitely the life. He crushed the box and chucked it onto the pile of rubbish. He'd get Jade to give him a trash-bag when she returned from babysitting Darya. Funny to think she was at his house while he was at hers. Or rather, on top of hers.

Bryn glanced at his watch. Two twenty. Hours to go until Jade returned. He considered his options. Another trip to the sauna? Maybe a workout in her parents' personal gym. Or some wide screen TV. He decided on the gym. Followed by a game of Space Bandits with Ned. Bryn was glad he'd brought the little machine with him. He'd toyed with the idea of burying it in the hole in his garden with the rest of his dad's stuff. For safety's sake. He knew now how important Ned was. But he'd changed his mind. A good decision. Ned was company.

Bryn opened the door of the small conservatory, stepped onto the flat roof. For a few minutes, he stared across the city. You could see for miles. Especially on a clear summer afternoon. Bryn stretched out a hand, palm flat, pretended to grab a passing cloud. He couldn't understand why Jade disliked living here so much. She had everything. Bryn had to keep reminding himself he was in hiding not on vacation. Jade's house was so luxurious, he could stay forever.

Jade carried a plate of linguine up to the roofgarden. She handed it to Bryn, then flopped onto the bench. She stretched out her legs, soaking up the late afternoon rays.

'Everything OK?' Bryn asked.

Jade nodded.

'You had a word with Gil, explained things?'

Jade nodded again.

'He's all right?'

'Yeah, fine.' He wasn't, but Jade understood. Bryn was Gil's best friend, she was an intruder. If it had been the other way around, she'd have resented it too.

'And Da?'

'Your sister's fine. Nobody's been round or tried to get in touch and I didn't see anything suspicious in the neighbourhood.'

Bryn let out his breath. 'So maybe I got it wrong after all. The warning was it. They're not following through.' He was surprised to find he felt almost disappointed.

'Seems that way.'

Bryn pulled a face. 'Looks like I'm heading home.'

'Uh-huh.'

'Shame. I was getting to like it here.'

There was a brief silence. Jade chewed thoughtfully on a fingernail. Then she remembered something: 'Oh yeah— Kirrin's coming round later,' she said.

'What—why?' Bryn was instantly on the alert.

'He's got something to tell you.'

'How'd he find out where I was?' Bryn asked.

'He saw me shopping yesterday. You know, buying two of everything. He guessed.'

Bryn swore.

'He'll be fine,' Jade reassured him. 'He promised he'd keep his mouth shut. And I believe him. Anyway, who'd he tell? He hasn't got any friends.' Jade couldn't help feeling a bit sorry for Kirrin. She knew he was having the worst time. She also knew what it was like to be the outsider. The one nobody liked.

'He could have told you whatever it was,' Bryn grumbled.

126

Jade grinned. 'He doesn't like me, he likes you,' she said. 'Be nice, Bryn. You should've seen what they did to him today.'

Bryn sighed. Frankly, Kirrin Neots rated a big zero on his care factor scale. Still, as it was Jade . . . 'OK, I guess,' he said reluctantly. 'Only you'd better be right about this.'

'Trust me,' Jade answered. 'You'll be fine. I promise.'

Kirrin could barely eat. He sat at the dining table, head lowered, pushing food around his plate. He so wanted to cry out 'suckers' to his father and his sister. At the head of the table, Mr Neots observed Kirrin closely. The boy was quite clearly hiding something, he thought to himself. It was patently obvious. The stupid idiot had the discretion of a warthog.

Mr Neots contemplated extracting Kirrin's secret by the usual method: bullying accompanied by beating. He decided to refrain. Let the boy think he was safe. Lull him into a sense of false security. Then, when least suspected, strike like a snake. He smiled to himself. Yes. That would make the revolting porcine creature jump. That would show him what happened to people who defied him.

Mr Neots secretly rubbed his hands together. He strongly suspected Kirrin's covert glee concerned the whereabouts of the boy Bryn. Well, he would bide his time. For now. Just so long as Kirrin didn't keep him waiting *too* long. His government contact was snapping at his heels for information.

Kirrin waited in his room until he was sure everybody was busy. Then he crept downstairs, opened the front door, and slipped silently out into the street. An instant later, Kallie bounded out of the living room and rushed across the hallway. She pushed open the study door.

'Kirrin's gone out,' she announced.

Mr Neots lifted his head from the pile of documents he was annotating. 'Yes, I heard him,' he said steadily.

'He didn't say where he was going. That's naughty.'

Mr Neots picked up his communicator. 'Don't worry, my princess,' he smiled grimly. 'We have ways of finding out exactly where he's gone.'

'Is he in big trouble, Daddy?' Kallie asked eagerly.

Mr Neots keyed in a number. 'Oh, I hope so,' he said. 'I really do hope so.'

Sigma

Kirrin hurried across town. He felt so important. He was on a mission: he was going to warn Bryn. Tell him that his father had been asking questions. Kirrin was happy. He thought Bryn had gone away. That he might not see him for ages. But he hadn't gone after all. Bryn was his hero, Kirrin thought. And now he had another chance to prove his loyalty and devotion.

Kirrin reached the gated estate where Jade lived. He was impressed. Big houses, sweeping driveways. Serious money. Then he realized he had a major problem. The gates were locked. He didn't know how to open them. Jade had forgotten to give him her passcode. Crestfallen, disappointed, Kirrin stood on the pavement outside, biting his lip and staring in through the bars. This was a major setback. He didn't know what to do.

A brand new ATV, the sort very rich people drove, drew up at the gate. There were two adults inside. The driver, an elegant middle-aged lady, lowered the window. 'Hello there, do you have a problem?' she asked pleasantly.

'I'm visiting a friend,' Kirrin told her. 'Only she didn't give me her code.'

'Who do you want?'

'Jade. She lives at number 51. You know her?'

'Jade! Oh yes,' the woman said. 'Hang on a minute— sorry, I don't know your name . . . '

'Kirrin,' Kirrin said.

'Kirrin, yes.' The woman leaned out, keyed in a series of numbers. The gates swung open. 'Thanks,' Kirrin called out, 'thanks a lot.' The woman waved cheerfully. The car moved swiftly away into the estate.

Kirrin walked until he reached Jade's house. He went up to the front door, rang the bell. As he waited, the garage door rose up to reveal the ATV. The couple, both carrying executive briefcases, emerged on to the driveway, deep in conversation.

'Who is it?' Jade's voice crackled on the intercom.

'Kirrin.' Kirrin spoke into the metal grid.

The couple crossed the immaculate green lawn.

'Hello again,' the woman said. 'Have you rung the bell?'

'Yeah—sorry, I don't understand?' Kirrin stammered.

'Introductions,' the woman said. 'I'm Ana and this is Mark. We're Jade's parents.'

'Right.' Kirrin shook hands with the tall, dark-haired man. Now he could see the resemblance clearly. Jade had her mother's deep gold-flecked brown eyes, her father's hair colour and tall, slim build. 'Pleased to meet you,' he said politely. He supposed they must know about Bryn.

The front door buzzed.

Jade's father pushed it open. 'Come in, Kirrin. Welcome to our home,' he said. He stood aside, letting Kirrin go in first.

Jade was waiting on the stairs.

Kirrin rushed up to meet her. 'Hi. Where's Bryn?' he asked eagerly.

Jade didn't reply. Instead, she looked past him at the couple now standing together on the doorstep, then glanced down at her watch. 'I don't understand; why are you both home now?' she asked wonderingly. The man and woman didn't reply.

Then suddenly Jade froze, staring at them over Kirrin's shoulder. 'Who are you?' she demanded.

'Huh?' Kirrin turned. The man and woman had entered

130

the house, closing the door quietly behind them. Duh, how stupid was she, Kirrin thought. 'Hello—they're your parents, remember,' he told Jade, tapping his forehead with one finger.

Jade made a strange animal noise deep in her throat. Kirrin looked at her. Jade's eyes were wide, dilated, fear-filled. The colour drained from her face. 'They're not my parents,' she exclaimed harshly. 'I've never seen these people before in my life.'

Suddenly, everything happened very quickly. Jade turned on her heel and fled upstairs screaming out a warning to Bryn. The woman dropped her briefcase and leapt forward in pursuit. She rushed up the stairs, pushing Kirrin roughly aside. Kirrin felt himself falling. He reached out wildly for something to cling on to. There was nothing. Then everything went black.

Bryn was just coming down from the roofgarden when he heard Jade scream a warning. He ran back, slammed the connecting door and bolted it. So they were here. It was really happening. Bryn's heart started racing. He checked round the parapet. No way down. Not unless he jumped. He contemplated this, then dismissed it. Too potentially fatal. The only way out was through the door.

Bryn darted into the small conservatory that had been his home for the last few days. He checked his watch. He reckoned he had a couple of minutes before they discovered him. He opened Ned's lid. The computer began its start-up ritual.

'No time,' Bryn exclaimed frantically. The fanfare and cheering ceased.

'Activate the daemon,' Bryn ordered.

Ned whirred busily. 'Daemon activated.'

'Thanks, Ned. Good work,' Bryn said. He might be

going down, but not without a fight. There was a loud banging on the door outside. Voices calling his name. Bryn tried to remain calm. He had to hide Ned. He looked around the untidy living space. Saw nothing. Bryn's heart did a backward flip. Why hadn't he buried Ned? Buried it deep in the earth with the rest of his father's things? Now it was too late. Suddenly, he spotted an old propagator on a shelf. He opened it, lowered Ned inside. 'Stay sharp,' he said quietly. 'I'll be back.'

The pounding upon the door became louder, rhythmical. The door was being kicked in. Bryn quickly stuffed the rest of his belongings into his rucksack, made a final check. Then he walked out of the shed, leaned against the parapet, and waited.

'You can't do this,' Jade exclaimed. 'We're world citizens, we have rights.'

The woman smiled. 'Nobody is infringing your "rights", Jade,' she said softly. 'All that is happening is you're making a little trip. Look upon it as a new and exciting adventure. A little outing with your parents.'

'You're not my parents,' Jade snapped back. She struggled to escape from the woman's tight arm-lock.

The couple exchanged amused glances. The man holding Bryn opened the front door. 'Would you like me to ask that man across the way if we're your parents?' he asked. Jade subsided, muttering swear words under her breath.

'Now, we can do this in a civilized way, or we can do it the way I prefer,' the man continued. His fingers dug viciously into Bryn's shoulder. 'You choose.'

Bryn winced. 'Civilized way,' he muttered.

'Wise choice,' the man said smoothly. 'Right. I'll get the ATV round to the front. Then you come out, nice and relaxed. Just pretend you're going on a picnic or something. OK?' He released his grip. Bryn rubbed the sore spot. 'Oh, and just to make sure that we all understand each other,' the man said over his shoulder as he went out, 'some of my friends are waiting outside. You can't see them, but they're there. And they aren't nearly as . . . reasonable as we are.'

Bryn waited until the man had left. Then he went over to the woman. 'Look,' he pleaded, 'you've got what you wanted. You don't need to involve her,' he nodded towards Jade. 'She's nothing. She's not part of this. Let her go. She won't tell anybody, I promise.'

Jade regarded him stonily. 'I *can* speak for myself, you know,' she snapped icily. She tried to kick the woman's shins. The woman held her at arms' length. Jade swore at her, eyes spitting hatred. The woman laughed. 'Little wildcat, aren't you?' she grinned. 'I feel sorry for your boyfriend.' She readjusted her grip on Jade.

'So you'll let her go then?' Bryn persisted.

The woman shook her head. 'No can do,' she said. 'Nice try but no deal. We've gone to a lot of trouble to set this up.'

'But she isn't . . .'

'You're both coming with us. He's decided he wants to see both of you.'

'He?'

The man appeared on the doorstep. 'The vehicle's outside. Let's go.'

Still holding Jade firmly, the woman propelled her along the hallway. 'What shall we do with him?' she asked, nodding at the still prostrate figure of Kirrin lying at the foot of the stairs.

'Neots's brat? Leave him,' the man shrugged, 'we're running out of time.' He beckoned Bryn forward. 'Come on, you. And remember what I said. No tricks. Or else.'

Bryn walked out. A big shiny ATV stood at the kerb,

its doors open. Without a word, he got into the back. Jade gasped. 'How did you . . . !'

'Get in!' the woman hissed. She turned, waved to an elderly man who was watering a front lawn. 'Hello, nice afternoon,' she called gaily.

'Going for a drive?' the man asked.

The woman nodded, pushing Jade into the rear of the vehicle. Jade leaned across her shoulder, 'Call the cops, I'm being kidnapped!' she yelled at the top of her voice. The woman slammed the door, then looked at the elderly man, shrugged her shoulders. 'Kids, eh!' she said good-humouredly, climbing into the driver's seat. Her partner got in beside her. The man laughed. Jade shrank into the corner, defeated, diminished. Her hands were balled into tight fists.

'You OK?' Bryn mouthed. Jade stared straight ahead. She wouldn't look at him.

The woman flicked the central locking into position, started the engine. The ATV drew away from the kerb, headed towards the gates. They swung silently open to let it through.

Kirrin opened his eyes. His head was throbbing. For a moment he lay still, wondering where he was. Then he remembered, struggled painfully to his feet. He listened. Silence. He called out Bryn's name. No answer. Kirrin's aching brain tried to sequence the events of the preceding hour. It failed. Dazed and bruised, he stumbled out of the house, stood forlornly on the driveway. He didn't know what to do.

'Looking for someone, son?'

Kirrin turned round. There was an old man in the opposite garden, rolling up a length of hosepipe. 'Uh, I was looking for Jade,' he said, vaguely.

'You just missed her,' the man told him. 'I saw her go a while ago.'

'Er . . . was she . . . on her own?'

'Seems like she had a friend with her.'

'And her parents?'

The man nodded.

'You sure they were her parents? I mean quite, quite sure?'

The man bridled. He glared at Kirrin. 'Son, I've worked around here for more years than you've lived on this earth,' he snapped indignantly, 'I know everybody on this estate. Known Mark and Ana from the day they moved in. Known Jade since she was born. I tell you, they all left a while back. In that brand new vehicle of theirs.' He muttered something under his breath, picked up the hosepipe and stomped round the side of the house.

Kirrin collapsed on the kerbside. He so wanted to believe the old man. Yet he had seen Jade's face. The terror in her eyes. The way she screamed out a warning to Bryn. But if that couple weren't her parents, who were they? Kirrin's head throbbed. None of it made sense.

And there was another thing: it was slowly dawning on his dulled and aching brain that in some way he was responsible for what had just happened. He had failed to warn Bryn. He had let himself be used by those people, whoever they were. He had exposed his only friend to danger. It was all his fault. Kirrin groaned. They would not forgive him. He'd blown it. When Bryn returned, he thought miserably, he'd never ever speak to him again.

Tau

The vehicle drove at breakneck speed out of town. Jade crouched in a corner like a wounded animal. She didn't speak, didn't move. Bryn regarded her anxiously. All the fight, all the spirit had left her. At one point on the journey he had tentatively put out his hand, touched her white-knuckled fist. Her skin felt cold, clammy. She had not responded to his touch. Now she seemed to have retreated within herself. As if she were listening to a voice that she alone heard.

They reached the outskirts of the city. Dusk was falling, rose-pink and lavender. The ATV swung right on to a field track. At the end of the track, Bryn saw a helicopter waiting, its blades rotating lazily in the fading daylight. The woman drove quickly towards it, stopped a short distance away. She turned off the engine. 'OK, out quickly, both of you!' she ordered.

Jade moved slowly, languidly, as if under water. Bryn took her hand, squeezed it comfortingly. 'We'll be all right,' he whispered. She did not reply. Bending low, he guided her across the brief space between car and helicopter. They climbed aboard. The doors closed. The helicopter lifted off the ground in one smooth movement, circled round so that it faced south.

Looking down, Bryn saw the man and woman peel off their disguises, take the fake plates off the ATV. Then they both got back in and drove away.

* * *

Mr Neots heard the front door quietly open. He counted under his breath: one . . . two . . . three . . . and flung wide his study door. As he had calculated, Kirrin was just about to enter the kitchen. Mr Neots folded his arms slowly, deliberately. It was a technique guaranteed to silence a noisy class in seconds. It worked again. Kirrin stopped, turned to face his father. Mr Neots noted the massive bruise on his son's forehead, the puffy, red-rimmed eyes, the marks of tears on his cheeks. And ignored them.

'So,' he said coldly, 'you have deigned to come back.'

Mute, miserable, Kirrin said nothing.

'And where, may I enquire, have you been all this time?'

Kirrin stared at him, an expression of fear and loathing on his swollen face. On the way home, it had begun to dawn on him that possibly he was not entirely responsible for what had happened to Bryn and Jade. His father must have played a fairly considerable part in it too. The unexpected arrival of Jade's 'parents' was a bit more than coincidence. Somebody had tipped them off. Kirrin had a strong suspicion who that person was.

Mr Neots drummed his fingers on his arm. Always a winning tactic. 'I am waiting,' he said.

'You know where I've been.'

Mr Neots's eyebrows shot up. 'I beg your pardon?'

'You heard,' Kirrin said. Suddenly, he felt totally weary, sick of it all. 'I've been to see Bryn. Can I go now, please. I want to get a drink, I've got a headache.'

Mr Neots held up a hand. 'Wait a moment. Let me get this straight: you say you've been to see Bryn—yes?' Kirrin nodded. 'But . . . ' Mr Neots's face took on an expression of innocently bewildered confusion, 'surely that cannot be true.'

'Yeah—like you'd know all about truth,' Kirrin muttered.

137

'I shall ignore that comment. The reason you cannot have seen Bryn is because he is not here. Bryn is on a school field trip.'

Kirrin's eyes widened. 'He isn't!'

Mr Neots sighed. He shook his head from side to side sadly. 'Kirrin, Kirrin. Why must you always lie and make life so unpleasant for everybody,' he said, going to the bottom of the stairs. He called to Kallie, who trotted out onto the landing in her pink PJs. 'Tell your brother where Bryn is, my angel.'

'He's on a field trip, Daddy,' Kallie piped.

'Are you sure, precious?'

Kallie nodded. 'His sister told me.'

'Thank you, Kallie. You may go back to bed now.' Kallie smirked, stuck out her tongue at her brother, and returned to her room.

Mr Neots turned to Kirrin, a smile of triumph on his thin face. 'Now do you see why you couldn't have seen Bryn. The boy is not here. So I repeat my question: where have you been?'

Kirrin was trapped. Whatever he said, he wouldn't be believed. If his father was involved in this, he had managed to cover his tracks completely and successfully. 'Uh, um, I don't know,' he stuttered.

'*Don't know?*' Mr Neots changed into heavily sarcastic mode. 'You've been out for several hours—without asking permission. You come in looking as if you've been fighting and you say you *don't know where you went*?'

Kirrin hung his head. He so wanted to grab some heavy object from the kitchen and smash it into his father's smug face.

'Go up to your room now!' Mr Neots barked.

'Can't I get a drink first?' Kirrin pleaded. There was a big metal meat tenderizer in the second drawer, he thought. Maybe he could grab that.

'Certainly not,' Mr Neots snapped. '*I* shall bring you up a drink. In due course. Then we will have a long talk about your behaviour.'

Wearily, Kirrin went up to his room. He knew what a 'long talk' meant. Usually not much talking. He shut his door, threw himself on his bed, burying his face in the cool pillow. It was so unfair. He'd done nothing wrong, yet he was being punished. He heard his father's heavy footsteps coming upstairs. Suddenly, Kirrin snapped. He leapt up, ran to the door and locked it. He turned up his music full volume and returned to his bed.

Kirrin removed his sheet, duvet cover, and pillow slip. He knotted them together. He opened his window, lowered one end of the line over the sill, knotting the other securely to the leg of his desk. He filled his pockets with sweets, then slid onto the sill, trying not to look down. Kirrin grasped the line, swung himself over the edge. The knot instantly gave way; Kirrin dropped like a stone.

He landed in a flower bed. He picked himself up, set off in the direction of Bryn's house. Once again, Kirrin was on a mission. This time, he was going to warn Bryn's mum. And this time, he was going to get it right.

The helicopter flew high above the land. Overhead, the sky darkened, stars appearing like random diamonds sewn on a purple cloth. I am seeing light from a million dead worlds, Jade thought. Down below, towns and cities were coming alive in street lamps, yellow pinpricks against a black background. I am travelling between life and death, she mused. It seemed to Jade that the distance was very small, almost insignificant. She and Bryn were even smaller and less significant. And yet they mattered. Someone had gone to a lot of trouble to set this up. Jade wondered who and why. She also wondered if her parents realized she was missing. Probably not.

The helicopter dropped down. Now Jade could see motorways with minute vehicles, their headlights tiny moving jewels. Then a ribbon of river, sinuous and black, fringed with brightly-lit buildings. They were coming in to land. The helicopter circled, banked steeply. It hovered above the vast rooftop of a white building. Jade saw the fluorescent landing H far below approaching, getting bigger. The pilot set down the helicopter smoothly in the centre. The blades spun frantically, then slowed. They had arrived.

Upsilon

The President's palace was a magnificent building. White, with marble pillars, it stood at the heart of the great capital city. It had its own beautiful landscaped gardens, surrounded by a high brick wall which was floodlit and razorwired. It was guarded day and night.

In summer, the ground floor was opened to the public. Visitors queued for hours to see the fine oak-panelled rooms, hand-woven carpets, the painted portraits of their President in elaborate gold frames. There were glass cases full of his awards for services to humanity, his medals for bravery and the honorary degrees awarded by numerous prestigious universities.

For extra money, visitors could have their pictures taken sitting at the vast mahogany desk with its scrolled legs and green leather top from where, a notice proclaimed, he ran the entire world.

It was all a big PR exercise. At the end of summer, everything was quietly packed up and put away. The ground floor went back to being an empty, nowhere place. An area of transit.

'Wait here,' the pilot commanded. 'I'll go tell somebody you've arrived.'

Bryn looked around. Bare walls, dirty floor with broken tiles. Dust everywhere. Nice place, he thought sarcastically. Impressive. Not.

'Where are we?' Jade asked. It was the first time she'd spoken since they'd left her house. The words echoed loudly round the empty room, making her jump.

'I think we're somewhere in the President's palace.' Bryn lowered his voice. 'Some part they don't open to the public.'

'Ugh!' Jade shivered. 'I don't like it.'

'Is it—you know . . . bad?' Bryn queried.

Jade nodded quickly. There was evil here. Dark shadows were forming and dissolving in her head. 'Have you got Ned?' she whispered.

Bryn shook his head. 'Hidden it.' His lips formed the words. 'Show you when we get back.'

'Are we going to get back?'

'They can't keep us here for ever. Our parents will notice.'

Jade smiled wryly. 'Maybe they've already put in two lookalikes,' she said. 'So nobody will realize we've gone missing. My folks wouldn't know the difference.'

And mine? Bryn thought. He felt a sudden sharp pang of longing for home. When this nightmare was over, he told himself, he'd make it up to them. He'd be nicer to Darya, help his mum a bit more. Maybe even tidy his room occasionally. He'd certainly stop taking everything for granted, start appreciating what he'd got.

The pilot returned. 'Follow me,' he ordered curtly.

Bryn and Jade walked behind him along a maze of dark corridors. Finally, the man stopped, opened two doors on opposite sides. He showed Jade into one room, pointed Bryn into the other.

'You're to stay in here, get some rest,' he told them. 'He will see you tomorrow.'

'He?'

The pilot shut the doors. Bryn heard the keys turn. Then the sound of footsteps walking quickly away. Then absolute silence. He felt for a light switch. Found none. The room was pitch black. Bryn sat down on the floor, his back against the locked door. Reality was starting to kick in. He'd been kidnapped. He was a prisoner. He was cold, tired, and a long way from home. Things were not looking good. And somehow he knew it was not going to get any better in the morning.

For the employees in Globechem, it was a simple procedure. One repeated almost mechanically at the start of every shift: log on, check internal messages. So the unsuspecting technician who logged on to his computer suspected nothing when he noticed an e-mail attachment marked 'Urgent message from Neots'. Sure, he had never come across the name before. But that wasn't a big deal. Globechem operated worldwide. And things had been unusually busy lately. Messages flying about between sites. A lot of crazy stuff going down. Maybe this Neots was some hotshot scientist from another part of the mighty Globechem empire, the technician thought. So he opened the file.

And activated the virus.

The man watched helplessly as files, data, vital documents, and years of research were gobbled up in micro-seconds. In no time at all, reports started coming in from networks all over the system. Globechem was under attack. Not from some remote cyber-geek, but from within the company itself. It had never happened before. And nobody knew what to do to stop it.

Within hours, the Globechem mainframe had crashed. People were screaming down communicators, sending frantic textmessages. Virus hunters were desperately trying to nail the bug's digital fingerprints. And the hapless technician who'd opened the original e-mail had quietly left the building and thrown himself under a passing truck.

* * *

Jade opened her eyes. Looked around. The room was bare, serviceable. A bed, the sort you got in cheap hotels, she thought. No bedding. A four-drawer filing cabinet with two of the drawers missing. Piles of empty folders on the floor. Slightly stale, musty smell. She had the definite feeling that this had been a storeroom up until last night. Somebody had shoved the bed in, hoping it would do.

Jade's watch said 9.30 in the morning. She swung her legs off the bed, got up. Her mouth felt dry, her face sticky and unwashed. She went to the door, started banging on it, shouting. Nobody came. Was she going to have to stay here for ever? She needed the toilet. Exasperated, she pounded on the door a bit more, yelling abuse. Then she seized the handle and twisted it violently. The door opened. Feeling slightly foolish, Jade ventured out into the empty corridor. There was a row of identical doors opposite. She knew one of them was Bryn's. And the others? Who knew what lurked behind those. For a moment, Jade hesitated. She was tempted to try her luck. Then she changed her mind. Prioritize, she told herself. Find a toilet. Wash. Get something to eat. Then come back and locate Bryn. So, trying to act as if she hadn't a care in the world, Jade set off to search out some basic amenities.

Bryn felt a steady pressure against his back. Somebody was calling his name. He moved away from the door. Jade pushed it open. She was carrying a carton of juice.

'Hi, you OK?' she asked. She handed him the carton. Bryn popped it open, tipped the contents down his throat.

Jade stared round the room. 'Geez, what a tip. I've got a bed in my room.'

'Lucky you.' Bryn wiped his mouth on the back of his hand.

'No bedding, though.'

'Uh-huh.' Bryn threw the empty carton into a corner. Stood up. 'Where'd you get that from?'

'Canteen. Two floors down. You want some breakfast? They've got rolls and stuff.'

'Maybe in a bit.' Bryn pointed to Jade's neck. She was wearing a chain. A small blue and silver disc hung off the end. 'What's that?'

'Oh yeah, I forgot.' Jade fished in her pocket, handed Bryn an identical chain. 'We have to wear them. Security.'

Bryn examined the disc carefully. 'Who gave you these?'

'The man,' Jade said simply. 'I don't know his name. He was the pilot last night. He says to be in the canteen in half an hour and he'll explain everything.'

'Oh?' Bryn tossed the chain up and down a couple of times. 'Good. I'd like to hear someone explain why we were kidnapped by two people pretending to be your parents. Why we were shoved into that helicopter and flown here. And why we had to spend the night locked in a store cupboard. Yeah, I'll be really interested to know the reason why all that happened.'

Jade shrugged. 'So are you coming or what?' she asked.

Bryn held out his hand. Jade stared, frowned. 'Huh?'

Bryn put a finger to his lips. 'The tag,' he mouthed, 'give me your tag.'

Still not understanding, Jade slipped the chain over her head, handed it over. Bryn dropped them both into a plastic bucket. 'Let's go,' he said, walking to the door.

'But . . .'

'Listen, do you want them to know exactly where we are, what we talk about?'

'You mean . . .'

'They were probably bugged,' Bryn said. 'But, hey, I feel far more ''secure'' now.'

Jade led the way down two flights of stairs. Bryn freshened up, then helped himself to a massive cooked breakfast in the canteen. Jade sat opposite. She watched him eat in disgusted fascination.

'That's better.' Bryn wiped the surface of his empty plate with a piece of bread. He pushed the plate away, glanced at his watch. 'Time to go.'

'We have to wait for the man,' Jade reminded him.

Bryn looked at her innocently. 'What man?'

This time Jade got the message. 'Where are we going?'

Bryn shrugged. 'We'll just move around. See what's going on. Then we'll slip out of the back while nobody's watching.'

The President's aide scanned the canteen area. The two kids definitely weren't there. He swore under his breath, spoke a couple of curt words into his wristmike. A voice answered. The aide swore again.

'What do you mean you've lost contact?'

The voice said something in reply.

'Well bloody find them. ASAP. And get them re-tagged. Use the microsyringe if you have to. I don't want them going missing again. We've enough on our hands with this other business.'

The President's aide closed his eyes. He needed this like a hole in the head. All morning frantic messages had been coming in from his opposite number at Globechem. He'd had a hard time keeping the news from leaking out. Even now, he knew that the best, most experienced virus hunters were trawling cyberspace looking for clues. They'd already located an address. It turned out to be a school. Meanwhile, the emergency anti-virus response team were trying to come up with antidotes. It was a mess out there. A complete bloody fiasco. But at least it wasn't his mess.

146

This, however, was. Right now, he knew he was potentially within a gnat's eyebrow of losing his job. Or maybe worse. Suddenly, the wristmike crackled into life. The aide listened intently.

'Yeah . . . yeah. About time. Right, this is what I want you to do . . . '

Bryn and Jade were running. Behind them, two black-leather-clad guards followed in hot pursuit. 'Down here,' Bryn yelled over his shoulder. He took a sharp left. Jade followed. She wished she was a bit fitter. Skipping Phys. Ed. had seemed a good idea at the time. Now, she was regretting it. The guards easily kept pace with them.

'Through here,' Bryn ordered. He pushed a glass door. They sprinted down a long white-painted corridor, turned a corner. It was a dead end. There was nowhere to run. Bryn looked around frantically. The guards were getting closer. He could hear their heavy breathing. Then he noticed the door. He'd almost missed it. It was painted white, same as the walls.

'In here,' he gasped. They ran inside. The door swung shut behind them. For a second or two, they stood hanging on to each other, gasping for breath. Then Jade let go of Bryn's arm, straightened up and looked around.

The room they had just entered was like a tropical rainforest. There were tall green-leaved trees, creepers, lianas. Birds flew in and out. Tiny gold-maned monkeys chattered and scampered through the branches. In the middle of the room, looking completely out of place, was a plain wooden desk. Behind the desk, sat an old man, busily writing something on a pad. His head was bent low in concentration. He didn't seem to have noticed he had acquired intruders.

Jade's eyes opened wide. 'Hey, this is amazing,' she murmured. She started walking towards the jungle. She hadn't spotted the man.

Bryn grabbed her arm, jerked her back. 'Quick, let's get out before he notices us,' he hissed nodding towards the seated figure. He turned round, pulling Jade along behind him. But the rainforest had somehow crept up behind them. So that now, where there had been a door, there were only gently swaying trees, twisty creepers, and bright squawking birds flying to and fro.

The President's aide spoke into his mike. 'Good work. OK you can both stand down. I won't be needing you any more.' He clicked the off button, went to get a cup of coffee. That had been easy, he thought. So easy. The aide knew the building like the back of his hand. Every twist and turn. It had been like herding sheep. He stirred some sugar into his coffee. Dumb kids! Still, at least they were no longer his problem. He grinned. Bet they thought they had escaped. They were about to find out how wrong they were.

Phi

T he President finished writing his note to himself. He looked up. His eyes, dark and glittering, peered out from beneath deeply hooded lids.

'Ah yes. Our guests,' he murmured. 'Please sit.'

Bryn and Jade looked around the room. 'There aren't any chairs,' Bryn said.

'No,' the President agreed. He chuckled. A sound like sandpaper rubbed on glass. 'It's a little joke, you see. A small trick. A jest. *There are no chairs.* So you have to stand.'

Jade stared at the jungle. 'Whoa,' she breathed. 'It's like something out of a dream.'

'Go closer. Experience for yourself,' the President invited expansively. As if in a daze, Jade wandered over to the edge of the jungle. She tried to touch a leaf. Her fingers went straight through it. She stretched out a hand towards one of the small golden monkeys. It bit her. 'Ow!' Jade exclaimed. She sucked her finger. The President watched, smiling. 'Ah well, there you are,' he murmured, 'sometimes dreams, sometimes reality. That's how it goes.'

He blinked a couple of times, turned to Bryn, 'Are you interested in philosophy at all?'

'What is this place?' Bryn stuttered, bewildered.

'This is my office. My little oasis of calm. My world within a world.' The President smiled broadly at him. 'Welcome. Welcome both of you.'

'Who are you?'

The President sighed. An expression of resigned sadness crossed his thin, lined face. 'I am most upset that you do not know,' he said, turning sideways so that he could only be seen in profile. 'Perhaps this may answer your question.'

'The President?' Bryn breathed. 'You're the President. But . . . '

'Admittedly the portrait you have grown used to is a little . . . well, shall we say flattering. Youthful maybe?' the President went on, looking at them quizzically. 'Yes. I see in your faces it is just so. Well, sometimes it happens that life mirrors art. And then again it doesn't. Which is clearly the case here. You're sure I can't interest either of you in a little philosophical discussion?'

Jade stared at the wizened figure behind the desk, her finger still in her mouth. Bryn moved nearer to her. 'Don't worry about this,' he murmured in her ear, 'but whoever this guy is, I think he's mad. Completely barking.'

'Oh, I think not,' the President said. Suddenly, his voice was completely different. Sharper, stronger. Menacing. Jade gave a little gasp, drew closer to Bryn. 'I think you may be mistaken there, Bryn,' the President went on, his dark eyes seeming to absorb every detail of Bryn's shocked face. 'But then you have made quite a lot of mistakes lately, haven't you?'

Bryn stared at him, open-mouthed.

'Let's see,' the President went on. 'On June 6th, you were seen hanging around one of my Globechem plants. On June 8th, you attempted to cut the perimeter wires— unsuccessfully, I believe. On June 12th, you were apprehended in exactly the same place at 2 o'clock in the morning, cautioned, and taken home in a police van. Am I right?'

Bryn said nothing in reply.

'I think I am right. Then we come to June 28th. On that day, you had a meeting with Professor Laud, one of my senior government advisers—alas now no longer with us.

After that meeting, and his highly unfortunate and tragic death, you made several attempts to contact him on a private and unlisted number. Please correct me if I am wrong.'

Bryn remained silent.

'You see, I really do know all about you.'

'Yeah?' Bryn exclaimed indignantly. 'So maybe you also know who arranged for my father to be killed? And Laud?'

'Bryn,' the President's voice was smooth as oiled silk, 'you know these things were accidents. Accidents happen all the time. Why can't you accept the truth?'

'Because it isn't the truth!' Bryn persisted. 'And they weren't accidents.'

'But I put it to you, who on earth would do such things?'

Bryn stared straight at him. 'I can't imagine. Maybe you know who did it?'

The President looked outraged. 'Oh dear,' he protested, 'I am shocked! As if I, the President of the world, would have knowledge of the criminal fraternity. What sort of a person do you think I am?'

'I don't know,' Bryn countered evenly. 'You tell me.'

The President's face lit up. 'Aha, a question upon the nature of existence. I knew you were interested in philosophy,' he said triumphantly.

Mr Neots glared round the room. This is the last time, he thought gleefully. The last time he would stand behind his desk, staring out at the rows of sullen, uncooperative faces. The last time he'd have to grade a pile of mediocre, uninspiring folders. In a few hours—a few short hours— no time at all really, he thought, freedom would fling wide its golden gates. He would stride through into a bright and glorious future.

'Today,' Mr Neots announced, 'we complete our studies of life in the twenty-first century . . . '

Complete. He paused to savour the word. He liked the finality of it. He glanced quickly round, checking. For once, everybody was working. Even the usual timeservers and misbegotten idlers had their heads down. Not that it would benefit them now. Too little too late. Mr Neots had already written their reports. They were not good. Oh no. He hoped their respective parents would make life very unpleasant for them.

'What can we look forward to in the future?' Mr Neots continued. He knew what he was looking forward to: freedom from the daily grinding drudgery of the classroom. An absence of children. Children. He shuddered. Procrastinating wastrels. They disgusted him.

'The future of this planet will be even more glorious than its past,' Mr Neots intoned. He didn't need to glance down at his notes. This was written on his heart. 'The President's ten year plan—copies of which can be accessed via the internet library—visualizes an earth completely regenerated. Already, we have reclaimed vast tracts of barren continents, eliminated world hunger, eradicated nearly all disease. In the future, men will inhabit the whole of the planet. Maybe even extend our territory into the far reaches of outer space. Our President has spoken of a united and harmonious universe. Under his great and benevolent leadership, we shall stride forward into the twenty-third century.'

He paused, savouring the power of his words. The bell sounded. The lesson was over. Mr Neots packed his books and walked out of the room. He did not make eye contact with a single student. He did not say goodbye.

The Head of Security waited outside the school. He was one happy cop. Every dog has its day and he was about to have his. In metaphorically canine terms, the Head of Security was a bulldog. But for years he'd been a leashed, muzzled bulldog, forced to keep his feet the right side of the bureaucratic line. He had not enjoyed playing 'yes sir/ no sir' whilst being patronized, belittled, and having the rule book quoted at him all the time. Now, the tables were about to turn. He was going to enjoy himself. He really was.

In the mirror, he saw Mr Neots emerge from the school building, walk briskly towards the gates. Gotcha! the Head of Security thought. He waited until Mr Neots drew alongside the car. Then he leant out of the window. 'Got a minute, squire?' he enquired casually.

Mr Neots stopped. 'Why, officer?' he asked coldly.

The Head of Security opened the passenger door. 'Just a little matter I have to clear up. Won't take much of your time,' he said sweetly.

Sighing deeply, Mr Neots got into the car. 'Yes?' he queried.

The Head of Security gunned the engine. 'Nice motor, this,' he remarked, pulling out into the traffic. 'Not had it long.'

Mr Neots fussed with his briefcase. 'What is this all about, officer? I really am busy.'

The Head of Security drove on. 'Must be hard work being a teacher,' he remarked equably.

'I am no longer a teacher,' Mr Neots snapped.

'No?' The Head of Security shifted an eyebrow imperceptibly. 'Must be hard work not being a teacher,' he amended.

Mr Neots glanced sharply at him, but the Head of Security's expression was impossible to read. The car arrived at the Globecop HQ. The Head of Security got out of the car. 'My office, squire,' he grunted, waddling into the building. Mr Neots hurried after him, shoulders stiff with indignation. Who did this petty jack-in-office think he was, he thought angrily. The man needed putting in his place. Firmly.

Mr Neots and the Head of Security faced each other across the desk. It was a scenario familiar to both of them. Now, however, the balance of power had shifted. Only one of them, however, knew this.

'Cuppa tea?' the Head of Security offered.

'No thank you.'

'Don't mind if I have one?'

Mr Neots inclined his head. The Head of Security went to get some tea from the machine. Let the bastard sweat, he thought. He took his time, chatted to a few subordinates, signed some timesheets. When he returned, he saw that Mr Neots was looking hot and uncomfortable. Oh dear, I really shouldn't have left him in an unventilated office on a scorcher like today, the Head of Security thought cheerfully.

'Nice weather we're having,' he remarked. He opened the window, turned on the air-conditioning.

Mr Neots ran a finger round the inside of his damp collar. 'This is outrageous!' he hissed. 'You inveigle me into your car. You keep me waiting in this miserable excuse of an office for hours! How dare you treat me like this! Do you know who I am?'

The Head of Security eased himself into his chair, unfolded a piece of paper. 'Well now,' he said slowly, 'according to this memo marked "Urgent and Extremely Important", you are: the dangerous computer hacker who knocked out the entire Globechem system.'

'What!!!'

'Of course,' the Head of Security continued amiably, 'I don't really understand these things. I'm what you might call a pen and paper man myself. As I always say, you know where you are with pen and paper.'

'*Are you out of your mind?*'

'Still, who am I to argue with the facts, eh?' the Head of Security went on imperturbably. 'Especially when I got it all here in black and white: *"a virus attacked the Globechem company in the early hours of this morning causing great damage. The virus blueprint was traced to an e-mail address, which turned out to be a school. Further investigation revealed that the virus's nickname, 'Neots', was the name of a teacher at the school"'.* The Head of Security looked up sharply. 'Your name, I think,' he said.

'But this is impossible!'

'Can't argue with facts, can you?'

'It must be some sort of joke!'

'Don't think they were laughing at Globechem.'

'It's a mistake. A trick,' Mr Neots floundered. 'Yes, that's what it must be. One of my pupils. They dislike me—I don't know why. They all knew I was leaving. Somebody's deliberately set me up. Yes, I know exactly the person: the boy Bryn. He's the one you should be questioning.'

'Ahead of you there, squire,' the Head of Security was relishing every moment of this, 'I've already been round his house. But his mother, a very nice lady, told me that at the time when the said offence was being committed, her son was away on a school trip.'

Mr Neots made a strangled sound.

'You feeling all right?' the Head of Security asked solicitously. 'You seem to have gone a funny colour.'

Mr Neots clutched the sides of his chair. 'I would like to go home now,' he said faintly, 'I am not well.'

'Aw . . . sorry to hear it,' the Head of Security drawled, shaking his head sympathetically, 'but I'm afraid I can't let you do that. More than my job's worth. Strict instructions from on high to keep you here.'

'But you can't,' Mr Neots protested, 'I have done nothing wrong.'

155

'I'm afraid I can. May I refer you to the Prevention of Cyber-terrorism Act,' the Head of Security informed him. 'Still,' he got up heavily, 'I'm sure he won't be long.'

'Who?'

'Your friend. The government minister. The one with the posh car. Didn't I say? Silly me—he wants to talk to you.'

Mr Neots uttered a groan.

'So if you'd care to accompany me,' the Head of Security opened the door of his office, smiled invitingly, 'I'm sure we can find you a nice cell to wait in.'

'*A cell?*'

'Won't be air-conditioned, of course. Sorry about that. After you, squire.'

Mr Neots tottered along the corridor. Behind him strolled the Head of Security, a broad, ecstatically happy grin upon his heavy-jowled face.

Chi

They had been given chairs. Jade carried out a thorough reality check on hers before sitting down.

Bryn said, 'So why are we here?'

The President steepled his long bony fingers. 'I will explain everything.'

I don't think so, Jade thought. Nobody who could really explain everything ever said that.

'But where to start?' the President mused. He closed his eyes, seeming to drift off. Bryn and Jade waited. 'In the beginning,' the President said, 'was the word . . . ' He paused, opened his eyes and looked from Bryn's face to Jade's in gentle enquiry. 'Now isn't that an interesting concept? I must ask you whether you ever thought about it?'

'Sorry,' Bryn said, 'but . . . '

'No. I see you have not. Pity . . . ' the President continued, ignoring Bryn's interruption. Once more his eyes closed wearily. Bryn looked at Jade, pulled a face, shrugged. The President's eyes reopened. 'Where was I?' he asked.

'The world,' Jade prompted, 'something about its beginning.'

'You mean the Big Explosion,' Bryn told him, 'that was the start of everything.'

The President gave him a sharp, low-lidded look. 'That's what you think happened, is it?'

'Of course,' Bryn said. 'Everyone knows the world

157

began when a rogue star exploded and millions of particles . . . '

The President waved a dismissive hand at him. Bryn stopped. 'I think you misheard me,' the President said. He closed his eyes again. 'In the beginning was the *word*,' he murmured softly, 'and the word was God.'

'Excuse me?' Bryn queried. He turned to Jade. 'What's he talking about?' he mouthed.

'No—hang on, I remember that name,' Jade said, 'we did it in second year history—monotheistic religions of the past. Yeah, it's coming back to me: in the old days, they used to think this ''God'' was the Supreme Being who created the world.'

The President inclined his head graciously. 'Quite correct. What a bright girl you are.'

'Yeah, but he didn't really exist, did he,' Bryn said scornfully. 'I mean, all that religious stuff—it was what primitive people believed in. Before they had proper science and technology. Now we know better. Nobody believes it any more.'

'Quite correct again,' the President agreed. He smiled. 'Why don't they believe it, do you suppose?'

Bryn shrugged. 'Never thought about it.'

'Exactly,' the President said triumphantly, leaning back in his chair. 'You never thought about it. Nobody ever thinks about it. Not any more. Once there was God, now there isn't.' He stretched his hand towards the jungle. A large and beautiful butterfly flapped its wings and flew towards him, landing on his outstretched palm. 'Now you see him,' the President murmured. He brought his other hand down quickly, imprisoning the insect. 'Now you don't.'

The President opened his hand. The butterfly had vanished. 'Yet what if somewhere, maybe, he continues to exist,' he murmured thoughtfully, staring at his empty palm.

158

Bryn and Jade exchanged bewildered glances. There was something strangely unsettling about the way the old man's moods kept changing. The way he jumped from one topic of conversation to another. There was no logical progression. It didn't make sense. They were becoming disorientated, losing their ability to react normally. The President viewed them covertly from beneath his eyelids.

'So let us recapitulate shall we?' he said, leaning forward and resting his elbows on the desk. 'Where were we? Oh yes—we were discussing the ancient and possibly erroneous theory that the world was created by God. Correct? Not on his own, of course,' he added, 'nobody could accomplish a job as big as that on his own. God had his helpers, his bright angels—you know what an angel is, don't you?'

'A divine messenger,' Jade said. 'A ministering spirit.' She stopped, frowning. She didn't recollect ever hearing the word before yet the definition had come into her mind from somewhere.

'Just so,' the President said. 'They made it all—the jungles, the rivers, the wildlife. Everything. In the beginning. And there was one special angel. Did you know that? I don't suppose you've ever heard of him? No. An angel of light. Helel—the shining one. The favourite. The one who was promised that he would someday inherit everything that was made. Until he was disinherited. Discarded like a piece of old rubbish to be replaced by another.'

What is he talking about now, Bryn thought exasperatedly. This is stupid. Why is he wasting our time with fairy tales. When are we going to be told why we're here? He looked at Jade to see if she felt the same way, but Jade was staring at the old man, entranced by his story.

'How do you know all this?' she asked.

The President gave her a sly look. 'I study history.'

159

'What happened to the angel?' Jade asked.

'He left. Mutated. Turned himself into a dark angel. He changed his name. From Helel to Lucifer. The Prince of Darkness. You see, without light there is only darkness. Without goodness, only evil.'

Jade shivered. 'Ugh. What happened to him after that?'

The President shrugged. 'Nobody knows what happened to him. Such a waste. He was so beautiful once. Like the world he helped to make.'

There was a silence.

The President opened his eyes very wide. 'Which people have destroyed,' he exclaimed loudly. 'So that now there is nothing left. No jungles, no rivers, no wildlife. Soon there will be no world. No people.'

'What?' Jade exclaimed. 'That's crazy—sorry,' she corrected herself, 'but look, we all know people did bad stuff to the planet in the past, but they stopped. We learned about it in school. The Regeneration of the Earth,' she turned to Bryn, 'back me up on this . . . '

'She's right,' Bryn said, 'it happened after the great cybercrash. People came to their senses, started rebuilding the planet.'

'Yeah,' Jade picked up, 'now there are programmes to replant, rebuild.'

'It's on the news every night,' Bryn added.

'That's why we recycle everything,' Jade said, 'use non-fossil fuel.'

'Renewable energy,' Bryn continued. 'No disrespect, but maybe you should get out a bit more. See what's really going on.'

The President sat motionless. He waited for them to run out of steam. Then he smiled viperishly. 'Ah, the credulous obedience of the masses,' he murmured. He opened a drawer in his desk, took something out, held it up. 'I'm sorry to disappoint you both,' he said quietly, 'but this is your world.'

'A computer disk?' Bryn exclaimed.

'Quite correct.'

'I don't get it.'

'No, I don't expect you do,' the President said equably. 'Why should you. It is, or rather has always been up to now, a closely guarded secret. You see, this is the Omega File.'

The Omega File.

It had been put into place after the world's computers had crashed, the President said. The Omega File was born out of chaos and disaster and despair. It had slowly evolved until now it ran everything on the planet. The Omega File monitored the weather, selecting appropriate conditions for the time of year. It could create wind, rain, and control the amount of sunlight reaching the earth by opening and closing a gigantic sky-filter. The Omega File contained images of the world as it used to be. These were used on TV programmes about the planet, to give the illusion that everything had got back to normal. ('It's always the same mangrove swamp, the same school of dolphins,' the President remarked, 'did you never notice?')

The Omega File's other primary function was to track and monitor information about every individual in the world. Thanks to the special software secretly planted in the hard-drive of all Globecomp machines, it had instant access to names, addresses, career details, everything. By cross-referring to other subfiles, it could throw up a lifestyle profile of everybody on the planet.

The Omega File knew who you were. It tracked where you went. It monitored when you shopped, what you bought, and how much you paid for it. It knew your family history, medical details, tax code, even the colour of your car. In the global monoculture, nothing was beyond its reach. All your movements and personal communications could be monitored and checked. To all intents and purposes, the Omega File controlled the world and everyone in it.

And the President controlled the Omega File.

Jade concentrated, trying to understand, even though her brain kept telling her she was so far out of her depth that the fish had lights on the end of their noses.

'So there you have it,' the President said. He rested his chin upon his cupped hands and smiled happily. 'I can see by your faces you are both terribly impressed,' he said.

Bryn looked dazed. He shook his head in disbelief. 'It's not true,' he murmured. He thought of long hot summer days, crisp frosty winter mornings. Had they really sprung out of a computer?

'Oh, it is quite true, I assure you,' the President said. He gave a chuckle which sounded like fingernails on a windowpane. 'Believe me, the world is a far less complex place than you imagine. Thanks to the Omega File, life has gone on perfectly for over a hundred and thirty years.'

But not for much longer.

The Omega File was failing, the President said. Recently, its response times had slowed dramatically. On a couple of occasions, it had almost crashed. It was also getting harder to access some of the more remote areas. The façade of normality was becoming impossible to sustain. The Omega File was running on empty.

'So you want help fixing it, right?' Bryn said, relieved. They'd taken a rather tortuous route to get here but at least he now understood what this was about. A simple computer problem. Now he knew where he was. For a moment back there, he'd been on the edge of scared.

162

'Ah, the impetuousness of youth,' the President observed drily.

'But you are going to fix it, aren't you?' Jade asked uneasily. Something about the President's nonchalant attitude and lack of concern was starting to bother her.

The President sighed. He cast his eyes up to the ceiling. Sun slanting through leaves threw stripes of light and shadow on to his body so that for a brief second, his face resembled something feral, a strange and sinister jungle creature. The only sounds in the room were birdsong and the shrill chatter of the tiny gold monkeys. Then: 'You know,' the President murmured thoughtfully, 'I *really* don't think I can be bothered any more.'

Kirrin tried the handle of his door. To his surprise, it opened. Cautiously, ears strained for any sounds, he tiptoed out onto the landing. Something must have happened, he thought. Something important. Why else was he being allowed out in between meals?

Kirrin had been locked in his room for two days. It was his punishment. In his haste to warn Bryn's mum, Kirrin had completely forgotten that Kallie's bedroom was next to his. Her window overlooked the garden too. Kallie had seen him escaping. She'd raised the alarm. Kirrin was recaptured by his father, taken home, and locked in his room. He was a prisoner in his own house.

Kirrin stood at the top of the stairs. Silence. He ventured halfway down. Then he heard something: a strange, choking noise. It came from the kitchen. He stumbled down the remaining stairs, pushed open the kitchen door, and stood transfixed on the threshold.

His mother was sitting at one end of the table, a glass in her hand. She was rocking back and forth, gasping and shaking.

'Mum?' Kirrin cried, running over and putting an arm round her. 'Mum, are you OK?'

Mrs Neots raised her eyes to her son's anxious face. Her eyes were bright with merriment. 'Your father,' she got out between gasps, 'has been arrested.'

Kirrin's mouth fell open. 'What?'

His mother's mouth quivered. 'They say he's a dangerous terrorist.' She raised her glass, emptied it in one swallow. Then she collapsed onto the table, helpless with laughter.

Kirrin stared at her heaving shoulders. What was going on? His mother extended the hand holding her glass. 'Get me another drink, son,' she said. Numb with shock, Kirrin went to the fridge to find a wine bottle.

'No, love, not wine. Just water'll do fine.'

'Huh?' Kirrin had never known his mum drink water. Ever. He ran the tap, filled her glass, and brought it back.

'Thanks, son.' His mum looked up at him. Kirrin saw, with shocked surprise, that underneath the hilarity, she was completely sober. 'You're a good boy. Look, I think there's some chocolate cake in the larder,' his mum went on. 'You help yourself. I reckon we both have things to celebrate, eh?'

Totally bemused by what was happening, Kirrin carried the cake up to his room. He loaded Freedom Fighters from Faran 4 on to his computer, then cut himself a big slice. Stuffing his mouth with sweet, gooey cake, Kirrin picked up the joystick and started celebrating.

Jade was losing all sense of time. How long had they been here? A few hours, a week? Nothing was making sense any more. Maybe the world as she knew it had already ceased to exist, she thought. Only this place remained. The rainforest and the two of them and the President.

164

Floating through space like some dark and malevolent star.

'Look,' Bryn pleaded, 'I'm good with computers. I could sort it.'

'Boy saves world?' the President said drily. 'I don't think so. No, I'm afraid the time has come to call a halt. Enough. Finis. The end.'

'But you can't do that—millions of people will die!' Bryn exclaimed. His sense of unreality was so strong that the thought crossed his mind that this wasn't really happening, that they had slipped into a parallel universe and the conversation was actually taking place somewhere else.

'Yes, indeed they will—eventually,' the President agreed. He picked up the large and very beautiful shell, started turning it over in his hand. 'Not straight away, of course. In theory, there will be a period of calm at first, while somebody tries to get control of the situation and fix the Omega File. They will be challenged by others who don't want their leadership and want to do things a different way—you see, I know how the human mind works *so* well. Then they will fight each other. By that time, there will be widespread disease and the food and oxygen will all have run out. *Then* everyone will die . . . '

Bryn heard Jade give a jagged gasp. Then in a low monotone, she chanted:

> *The first horse is white and a king rides upon it*
> *The second is red, the colour of blood.*
> *The third is black and famine follows it*
> *The fourth—'*

Bryn stared at her. Jade clapped her hands over her mouth, the colour draining from her face. What had she said? The words had spilled out before she could prevent them. The President turned sharply to look at her. His eyes glittered under their deeply hooded lids. He looked like a snake poised to strike.

'The fourth?' he enquired softly.

Jade felt her face going scarlet with embarrassment.

'Tell me about the fourth horse, Jade?' the voice was gentle, coaxing. It probed.

Jade shook her head. 'It's nothing. A stupid nightmare I get sometimes. It's not important.'

The President went on staring at her. He's trying to get into my mind, Jade thought. She could see pale, almost transparent fingers extending from his head, reaching out towards her. Jade fought for control. She forced her gaze away, fixing it upon her lap. She dug her nails into the palms of her hands until the pain wiped the images of hooves striking sparks on cobbles, the sound of jingling harness. When she looked up again, everything was back to how it was before. He's dangerous, Jade thought. Very, very dangerous. And yet she didn't feel fear. Fleetingly, Jade wondered why she was not afraid.

Bryn shook his head slowly. Coloured horses? Kings? What was she on about? He had forgotten how weird Jade could be. He glared at her. Now what was she trying to do? Stare down the President? What was she hoping to achieve? He made another attempt to get things back on track even though his disbelief was currently suspended so far it was screaming out for extra rope.

'The Omega File,' he said, 'do you know how much longer it's got?'

The President consulted his watch. 'Four hours and twenty-three minutes exactly,' he said calmly.

'Huh?'

'The Omega File will start to fail at precisely six minutes past six o'clock this evening.'

'What?!! But you said it would take some time.'

'I said *in theory*,' the President replied calmly. 'In practice, however, it will fail shortly after the time I have quoted to you.'

166

'How can you know that for sure?' Bryn cried.

'Because that is the exact time that I and my companions will be leaving the earth.'

He's lost it, Bryn thought. He fought his rising panic. Stay centred, he told himself. Humour the old guy. Maybe this is some sort of trick. A peculiar endurance test. Maybe any minute now the door will open—trees will part, he corrected himself, and we'll be on some TV gameshow winning prizes.

'OK, so you're leaving, huh?' Bryn said in the calm voice of one trying to be reasonable while madness is hacking at the door with a large machete. 'And . . . uh . . . are you going somewhere special?' The President gave him a shrewd look. He knows, Bryn thought helplessly. He senses I'm bluffing. He can tell I'm afraid.

'That's an interesting question,' the President said. He leaned back in his chair, steepled his fingers. 'I'm so glad you've decided to ask an interesting question at last. I was just beginning to think I might be getting bored.'

Bryn glanced at Jade hoping for some helpful input. But Jade was staring fixedly at the rainforest. She appeared to be taking no part in the conversation. He was going to have to cope alone.

The President closed his eyes:

'*Then I saw a new heaven and a new earth, for the first heaven and the first earth had passed away,*' he said. He paused, opened his eyes slightly. 'Well, there you are. Now you know.'

'Excuse me?'

'The answer to your question: where am I going.'

'A new heaven? A new earth?' Bryn repeated dazed.

'Correct. You seem surprised. Why? Did you think there was only one?'

'Are we talking God and his bright angels again?'

The President inclined his head graciously. 'Indeed we are. There was always going to be a second world, a better one. A back-up location. A reward for all the people who believed in him. Somewhere for them to go once they quit this world.' The President pulled a disgusted face.

Bryn tried to focus. Another earth? Was it possible? He knew quite a lot about the solar system from science class. More from the computer games he'd played. There was never any suggestion that such a location existed. Even in the dubious unreality of cyberspace.

'This other earth,' he said slowly, 'where is it located? Do you know its exact co-ordinates?'

The President's face darkened. He emitted a snarl of anger. 'I knew once! Long ago, when I was . . . before I became . . . ' Suddenly he slammed his fist on the desk making Bryn jump. 'If I knew where it was, do you think I'd still be here?' he shouted.

'So you're stuck then, aren't you!' Bryn exclaimed triumphantly. 'Until you find out where you're going, you can't go anywhere.' Now he knew the old man was totally mad. All this talk about destroying the earth and escaping to a new planet was pure speculation, complete fantasy. He was listening to the ravings of a warped and very peculiar mind.

'Oh, I shall know very soon,' the President said. He seemed suddenly calmer, more in control. A smile of infinite cunning flicked across his thin, bloodless lips. 'And then we will be on our way. It will not take long to get there; my scientific research team has finally come up with a totally new fuel that will cut the journey time by two-thirds.'

Suddenly, something clicked in Bryn's mind. He remembered what Laud had told him about the secret research being done at Globechem. Rocket fuel. So that was what had been going on in secret.

'It has been an interesting experiment, ruling the world,' the President went on, 'but it is interesting no longer. It is time to close it down and move on. That is why I and my followers are getting out. I am going to invade the new earth and take it over. I am armed and ready. My spacefleet contains weapons of mass destruction capable of spreading terrible diseases for which there is no known cure.'

The Globechem file Ned had copied, Bryn thought. Anthrax, typhoid: weapons of mass destruction. Now it made sense.

'We will take the new earth by surprise,' the President went on calmly. 'He will not be expecting us. He is not armed, I know that for a fact. He will have no time to prepare any resistance. We will succeed. I have only been waiting for the exact co-ordinates, the precise location. And I shall shortly have them in my possession.'

Bryn was finding it impossible to keep a grip on reality. Every time he thought he understood, it slid away from him. He was being sucked into mental quicksand. In desperation, he turned to Jade for help. But Jade's chair was empty. She had vanished.

Psi

Agentle breeze ruffled the edges of the leaves. The golden monkeys leapt and chattered warnings to each other. Bryn got up. He looked around, called 'Jade?' But Jade was not in the room. Bryn started running frantically round, searching for the way out. His hand passed through trees, creepers, touched solid wall on all four sides. There was no door.

The President watched him detachedly, silently.

Finally Bryn gave up, returned to his chair and covered his face with his hands. 'I can't handle this,' he groaned. 'Nothing's making sense.'

The thin, sharp voice cut into his despair. 'On the contrary, Bryn. It all makes perfect sense. Let me explain things to you simply. You are going to stay in this room until I and my companions have gone. As soon as we have safely left Earth, some of the disease-carrying weapons will be released into the atmosphere. Then I shall initiate the destruction of the Omega File. Everything will fail. Everybody will die.'

Bryn stared at the old man with shocked eyes. 'But I don't understand—why are you doing this?'

'Why not?' the President replied calmly. 'You're all going to die very soon anyway. The earth can't sustain life much longer. In a way, I'm really doing you a big favour. And I have other . . . how shall I put it . . . more personal reasons.'

'And Jade?'

Instead of answering directly, the President bared his thin wrist. 'Look,' he said, 'do you recognize this?'

Bryn peered at it. There was a faint tattoo—a set of numbers. 'The numbers—they're the same as Jade's security code.' He looked at the President. Dark, cold brown eyes, the colour of dead leaves in winter, stared back. Bryn remembered what Jade had told him about her origins. The baby-making clinic. You chose a father . . . Suddenly, the chilling truth hit him. 'But that means you're her . . . '

The President waved a dismissive hand. 'The word means nothing to me,' he cut in, his voice flat, unemotional. 'Her only importance is the information she carries in her head. That is why she is here. You see, Bryn, when I realized my body and my mind had started ageing and I was beginning to lose those things that were important to me, I decided to reinvent myself, as it were.

'Each child I "fathered" carried my genetic make-up. So I knew there was a chance that one might carry in their head the knowledge that was slipping away from me. One of them had to know the location of the new earth. Jade isn't the first; there have been others. Over time. Many, many others. I have monitored each one carefully but none of them has ever shown any sign of possessing it. Until Jade. The last child. The solitary one. The dreamer of dreams. Have you noticed how completely unlike the rest of you she is?

'I have had her watched as she grew. And today my hopes have been realized. As soon as she mentioned the four horsemen, I knew she was the one who possesses the location. If she knows about them, then the information is there too, encoded in her mind, even though she doesn't realize it.'

'But I don't understand,' Bryn stammered. 'Who are these horsemen?'

The President looked at Bryn's uncomprehending face. 'The horsemen are the sign that the end of the world is

171

near. Their coming has been foretold from the beginning. When people stopped believing in God, they lost the knowledge of their existence. Now it is too late. The horsemen will initiate the final phase: mankind's last battle for life or death.' The President paused. 'Which mankind will lose,' he went on quietly. 'Only somebody whose mind can see the beginning and end of things, the time before and beyond time would know of them. Jade is the chosen one. She is the reason you are here.'

'*Jade* is the reason?' Bryn gasped.

The President gave him a pitying look. 'Oh dear—did you think this was about you, Bryn? Yes, I see from your expression that you did.' The President's voice was cold, his face like a death mask. 'It was never about you, Bryn. Sorry to disappoint you. It was always about her. From the moment she was born. She is my passport to a new life. Whereas you, Bryn, just happened to get caught up in things. In reality, you are completely unimportant, irrelevant. Just like your father and that stupid Professor Laud.'

Bryn stared at him, stunned-eyed. The President picked up the beautiful shell, gripped it with both hands. There was a sharp cracking sound. The shell splintered into a thousand pieces. The President looked from the broken fragments to Bryn and back again. 'A lesson for you, Bryn,' he said quietly, 'a metaphor. An analogy. Do you understand?'

White-faced, Bryn nodded. Finally, he understood everything. 'Where is Jade?' he asked, his voice shaking.

'The girl has been taken to have her mind extracted and decoded,' the President replied calmly. 'She is probably dead by now. Whatever happens, you will never see her again.'

Bryn felt an icy shiver run down his spine. Suddenly he knew he was face to face with a power that was infinitely old and deeply evil. '*Who are you?*' he whispered.

The President smiled. 'Haven't you realized it yet? I am the dark angel. I am Lucifer.' He got up from his seat. 'Goodbye, Bryn,' he said, 'and don't worry, dying is just a change of direction.'

Then he walked into the rainforest and disappeared.

Omega

J ade was travelling. The journey started with a butterfly. She remembered the butterfly. It landed upon a leaf, right by her shoulder. So vibrantly beautiful. She had followed the butterfly through the rainforest to a place where . . . and then . . . Jade frowned. That part was a bit vague. Now she was walking along a road.

The road was straight and empty. Jade didn't know where it was heading, only that she was going its way. So she walked. It was very strange and silent. The only sounds were her footsteps. Maybe this is a dream, Jade thought. But could it be a dream if she was able to think about it so logically? Dreams were more random, less purposed. At least hers usually were.

Jade thought of ways to prove to herself that this was in fact reality. She could pinch her arm, deliberately stub her toe. She could make the decision to turn round and go back. She could do all these things and more. But there seemed little point. She was here. The road stretched in front of her. She went on walking.

After a while, Jade saw something in the distance. At first, it was just a pale glow upon the horizon. Then it took on a shape, an outline. Jade saw tall buildings that shimmered, rooftops glowing like burnished gold in the pure light. She had reached a great city. As she got closer, she saw that it was surrounded by a high wall.

Jade walked slowly round the walls, looking for a way in. There were gates. She counted twelve. But they were all closed and there was nobody to help her. Jade sat down close to one of the gates. She leaned against the wall. It felt warm, as if the sun had recently shone upon it. There didn't appear to be any night or day in this place, but her inner clock told her it was time to sleep. Perhaps when she woke, somebody would be there to let her into the city.

Jade tried to focus her mind back. Why was she here, she wondered sleepily. What had happened? There was a road. She remembered that. And before the road . . . ? She tried to recollect what had happened before the road. But there was nothing. An empty space. She could not remember a single thing. She curled in closer to the wall, letting the warmth fill her and comfort her. It was very quiet, very peaceful. She felt her eyes closing, her body floating away upon a calm and tranquil sea.

Jade slept.

Mr Neots had seen his government contact in many moods, many roles. He had, however, never seen him in a mood like this. If he'd thought it was bad enough being cooped up in a stifling, airless cell, that was nothing compared to the stream of invective being aimed at him by the big, smart-suited individual he'd always thought of as his particular friend and ally.

'What I don't understand,' the man shouted, thumping the table with a large, well-manicured hand, 'is how you could be so unbelievably STUPID!!'

'But I keep telling you,' Mr Neots bleated, 'it wasn't me. This is all a terrible mistake!'

'After all I did for you,' the man continued, waving aside Mr Neots's protest as one might a troublesome fly, 'and *this*, THIS is the way you reward me!'

Mr Neots winced painfully. 'I do assure you, I will do everything in my power to rectify the situation,' he said, submissively.

'Oh, it's far too late for that now, Neots. Thanks to you, the damage has already occurred.'

'Damage?'

'As a result of your little stunt, a very important project, due to be implemented this evening, has had to be delayed by several hours.'

Mr Neots quivered. 'I don't know what to say; I can only apologize,' he said, wringing his hands.

The man gave him a withering look. 'Yes, so you keep doing. And to very little effect.' He rolled his eyes, shook his head sadly. 'Well, I'm afraid that as far as any further connection between us goes, that's it.'

'That's it?' Mr Neots gasped.

'Oh, come now, Neots, you can hardly expect me to still offer you a responsible government post after your name is splashed across the papers and on the TV news. I mean to say,' the man laughed sardonically, 'what sort of impression of the government would that create?'

'But . . . but,' Mr Neots spluttered, 'I was promised a job. What am I going to do? I have resigned my teaching post. I must work somewhere.'

The man paused, seemed to consider his problem. 'There is one position I could make available,' he said at last, stroking the side of his chin thoughtfully with one finger.

'Anything, I'll do anything,' Mr Neots begged.

'The water treatment plant needs another worker. I suppose I could recommend you for that.'

'Water treatment plant?' Mr Neots choked, horrified. 'But that's . . .'

'Sewage, yes. They want a shit shoveller, Neots. Why? Got a problem with it?'

Mr Neots swallowed hard. He gritted his teeth. 'No, not at all,' he mumbled faintly.

'Good. I'll set it all up for you then.' The man glanced

down at his large, expensive gold watch. 'Right. I can't waste any more time. I have to hurry back to the city,' he said briskly, striding to the door. Mr Neots slumped in his chair, covering his face with his hands.

The man looked at him, a knowing smile lurking around his lips. 'Cheer up, Neots,' he said, 'after all, it's not as if it's the end of the world.'

Jade opened her eyes. She uncurled, yawned, and stretched. She got up. How long had she slept? She consulted her watch but was unable to determine the answer: it had stopped. Jade looked up at the smooth, vertically opaque sides of the city wall. How had she arrived here? She tried to remember but her mind was a complete blank. There was only now. Nothing else existed.

The walls of the city sparkled in the brilliant white light. The air was so pure and clean that Jade felt almost lightheaded. Perhaps that was also why she didn't feel hungry or thirsty. She tried the gate a second time. It was still shut. Undeterred, Jade sat down in front of it, curling her arms round her knees. She waited patiently for somebody to come.

Everybody needs their own space. Jade's was generally located inside her head. Except that now, she was sharing it with a voice. Every now and then, the voice spoke, parting the silence. *You can choose, you know,* was its latest contribution.

Jade was quite interested in the voice. At first, she thought it had an echo. Now, she'd decided it was not an echo at all. More a plaiting of voices.

'Who are you?' she asked it.

'*I am Alpha and Omega,*' the voice replied enigmatically. '*Decide. You have choices.*'

The voice did not seem to have any bodily origin. Yet when it spoke, there was an effect of filled space.

'What's your name?' Jade asked.

'*I am the first and the last,*' the voice informed her. '*To stay or go. It's your decision. Take your time.*'

Jade repeated the words in her mind. To stay or go. Somehow, these were concepts she no longer recognized. She fixed her eyes upon the gleaming city gates. She knew that they had been put there for a purpose. But she couldn't exactly remember why she was there. Her mind was shedding itself of the past. Everything was steadily slipping away, the boundaries of her brain edging inwards. Now there was just the voice. And a sense of confusion.

'What are you called?' Jade asked.

'*I am the beginning and the end,*' the voice told her. '*Is there a problem?*'

I can't decide, Jade thought, I don't know how to make choices any more.

As if reading her mind, the voice said gently: '*Look . . .*'

Jade looked. The gate of the city seemed to become more opaque, until she could see through it. She saw broad streets, white buildings radiating soft golden light. A river lined with trees that dipped their fruit-laden branches into its sparkling crystal water. It was so beautiful, so peaceful. She saw people walking about. They were wearing long white robes and their faces seemed to shine. Jade felt a sense of deep happiness and contentment. She got up, took a step forward.

'*Wait: . . . there is another choice,*' the voice cautioned.

The vision faded. Suddenly, Jade saw clearly for the first time what she had only ever seen in shadows or in dreams. She saw the four horsemen riding out across the world, silent and purposeful. She saw the figure on the white horse raise his arm and at his signal, the red rider drew his sword from its sheath. Then Jade heard once again the frightening sounds of battle, the clashing of great armies, the screams of wounded men. Now the black horseman raised his arm, and as she watched, the sky seemed to close up so that there was no sun or rain. And she heard the agonized sound of people crying for food and water as they starved. Finally, the fourth rider stretched out his arm over the world and in his pale face, she saw Death.

'No,' Jade whimpered, 'please, no more.' She shut her eyes, stuck her fingers in her ears to block out the terror and anguish.

'*It is not yet over . . .*'

Then Jade saw a face superimposed upon the darkness behind her eyes. At first, she did not know who it was. Then she realized it was Bryn's face. Jade remembered how Bryn had befriended her, looked out for her. How he had cared for her when nobody else did. She visualized him, left on his own in that weird room. She entered into his pain and despair. Suddenly, the terror that had engulfed her faded away and she felt only a heart-cutting sadness. All at once, she knew she couldn't leave Bryn on his own. Not after all he had done for her.

Jade made her choice. 'I want to go back,' she said. The voice made a corporate noise of acceptance. 'But I don't know what to do,' she went on. 'And,' she admitted, 'I'm really scared.'

'*We give you courage and wisdom,*' the voice said. Jade heard the whisper echo: 'courage and wisdom . . . courage and wisdom.' She felt something touch her face delicately, like the breath of a bird's wing. Then the light began to fade around her and she felt herself gently falling backwards into darkness.

Thick black surrounded her, clung to her. Jade was curled on her side, knees drawn up to her chin, tightly trapped like

179

an unborn child. She couldn't breathe, couldn't move. Desperately, she gasped for air, kicking out and clawing with her hands. There was a jagged tearing sound. Daylight and fresh air rushed in. Jade sat up, looked around. Where was she? What was this place? Then she realized: she was in a dumpster. Someone had put her body in a black bin bag and thrown her away like a piece of unwanted rubbish. Jade was outraged. Swearing loudly, she clambered out of the dumpster, brushing away the settling flies. She was at the back of the President's palace and it was late afternoon, humid, with the threat of thunder in the air.

Jade strode round to the front, slipping unnoticed through a gap in the railings. She had a plan. The area outside the palace swarmed with tourists clutching maps, taking videopics. Down one side was a line of cabs waiting for customers. Jade walked over to the lead cab. 'Can you take me home?' she said. She gave the driver her address.

The man looked her up and down. Jade's hair was matted and filthy, her clothes stained and crumpled. She smelt bad. The man waved a dismissive hand. 'Getchaself a life, garbage-girl,' he grinned. Jade pressed a number on her watch face. 'Look,' she said, showing the man, 'this is how much I've got in my bank account right now.' The man glanced at the tiny display and gasped as the cumulation of several years' unspent clothes allowance flashed onto the minute screen. 'Sheez!' he swore, staring doubtfully at Jade. 'You fer real?'

Jade nodded. 'You can have it all,' she promised, 'if you'll get me home as quickly as possible.'

The man thought fast. He looked at Jade again. Then he opened the rear door. 'OK, little sister. You gotchaself a ride,' he said, 'only, hey—couldya try not to mess up tha cab?'

*   *   *

180

Night was falling when they pulled up at the gates to the estate. Jade transferred the money over. The cab drove off. Jade opened the gates, then let herself into her house. Resisting the temptation to freshen up and change out of her filthy clothes, she went straight to the roofgarden. Stay focused, she told herself. First things first. Prioritize.

Jade sat on the ground, the square black box on her lap. Gingerly, she lifted the lid.

'Hi, Ned,' she said.

There was a ripple of sound. The screen lit up. Jade took a deep breath. Bryn had told her about Ned and its attitude problem. She wasn't totally sure she could deal with it. But she knew she had to. Courage and wisdom, she reminded herself. She was going to need them, she thought grimly. 'Er . . . it's me, not Bryn. Sorry,' Jade said. There was a pause while Ned appeared to think about this. Then, to Jade's astonishment, it responded in a female voice: 'Hello, dear. What can I do for you?' the voice said. It was sort of motherly with bossy edges.

'Oh . . . umm . . . err,' Jade fluffed.

'Could you be a bit more specific, my love?'

Jade struggled to express her thoughts logically. 'I want you to break into a computer system which is probably on a spacecraft,' she told Ned. Even as she spoke, she realized how stupid this sounded. What on earth had possessed her? Stupid, stupid! She should've obeyed her first instincts and tried to get back into the palace, then locate Bryn. He'd know what to do.

Meanwhile, Ned remained ominously silent, its screen blank.

Jade sighed. 'OK, sorry. Forget it,' she said, 'I never really thought you could do it in the first place.'

'EXCUSE ME!' the female voice bristled with indignation.

'Huh?'

The computer muttered under its breath about impatient young people who couldn't wait two seconds etc., etc.

'Can you do it?'

'Given the CORRECT data, it may be possible,' the computer said sniffily. 'So far, that has not happened.'

'So what do you need?'

'The launch site would be a start,' the computer said. Did it sound fractionally less huffy? 'There may be a tracking program in operation. I could enter the main system that way.'

Jade pulled a face. 'I don't know where it was launched,' she admitted, 'but if you can get into the computer system in the President's palace, we might find out.'

The computer whirred and chuntered to itself. Long series of numbers and letters scrolled up the screen. Jade watched. She held her breath, hoping that everything Bryn had told her about Ned's ability to break into systems was true. At last the words: *System reached. Please enter password*, flashed up. Jade's mind blanked. She hadn't a clue what to do next. Wisdom, she thought. I need wisdom. She concentrated. Waited for an idea to arrive. Nothing happened. Finally in desperation, Jade typed in her own ID code—the triple six combination she used to activate the estate gates. The computer processed this. Then the screen flashed: *Password accepted*. Jade gaped at it in amazement. She'd not seriously thought in a million years it would work.

'Hey, brilliant. We're in,' she breathed.

'Maybe, but there are *a lot* of files to scan,' the computer said pointedly.

'OK.'

'The operation may take some time.'

'Right. So?'

There was a pause. The computer sighed. 'Haven't you got any homework to do?'

Jade took the hint. She set Ned down on the ground. 'Er . . . you couldn't hurry it up, could you?' she asked, scrambling to her feet.

The computer grumbled away to itself. Jade ignored it. She stretched, filling her lungs with warm, scented night air. Up on the roof, it was very quiet. As though the whole world was holding its breath, waiting . . .

Jade went quietly into the bathroom, turned on the shower. She dumped her dirty stuff in the laundry basket, then let the hot water soothe away her cares. So far so good, she thought. She wrapped herself in a big, fluffy bath towel and tiptoed along the corridor to her bedroom.

Somebody was asleep in her bed. Jade stared at the dark-haired girl and snorted in disgust. Pathetic, she thought. She looks nothing like me. And I never go to bed this early! Moving carefully so as not to wake the sleeping lookalike, she helped herself to fresh clothes and crept out of the room. The fake Jade was going to have problems explaining the filthy clothes and the mess in the bathroom!

She returned to the roof.

'Back already, dear?' the computer observed. 'Finished your homework?'

'Yeah,' Jade lied, sitting down.

'Tidied your room?'

'Yeah. Have you found the spacecraft?'

'I have established contact with the onboard computer,' Ned said smugly. 'It was not difficult. There was no security system in operation at all.'

No, Jade thought grimly. There wouldn't be. He wasn't expecting any opposition. She visualized the President at the controls, secure in the knowledge of his safety.

'I cannot maintain contact for long,' the computer went on, 'the spacefleet is leaving the earth's atmosphere.'

'Right,' Jade acknowledged. She thought swiftly. 'Can you plant a program—something that will destroy it.'

'Of course I can, dear,' Ned said affably. There was a microsecond's pause. 'The virus is now uploaded. Would you like to give it a name?'

Jade nodded, then hesitated. This was so big, so important that it seemed inappropriate to call it after herself or Bryn. But Ned was right; the virus needed a name. Evil and darkness should not just fade away anonymously, she thought. It had to be destroyed in the name of something. Or someone. Once again Jade saw the face of the President, gloating triumphantly over the dying world he had once controlled, then abandoned. Then she remembered the beautiful city full of light. She recollected the voice she'd heard in her mind. She focused upon the voice. And as if it had been waiting for this moment, a name came into her head. Jade typed it, then pressed the enter key.

'The virus is activated,' Ned said.

Everything was stilled and silent; time skipped a heartbeat.

Suddenly Jade felt a spasm of pain ripping through her body. She fell to the ground, gasping, crying out.

Then: 'The spacefleet has been destroyed,' Ned announced calmly.

Streetlights spilled yellow pools onto midnight pavements. Jade walked past sleeping houses, along silent, empty streets. She carried Ned under one arm. She was returning to the city. She was taking the little computer back to Bryn. Jade reasoned that if Ned could destroy, it could also rebuild. It was logical. So Ned could repair the Omega File.

Ned and Bryn together. And after that, they could all start work on the earth itself.

Jade reached a corner, stopped and listened. In the distance she heard the roar of traffic on the motorway. And somewhere, hovering in the night air, she could just make out the faint rhythmic sound of horses' hooves. Faint and growing fainter until almost on the edge of hearing, they faded away into the night, leaving only darkness and silence behind them.

The horsemen had gone.

Jade felt suddenly light and free. 'Girl saves world,' she thought, grinning. It sounded good. She walked on until she reached the area of town which was close to the motorway. She knew there were always trucks going south, even this late at night. She would pick up a ride easily.

Jade crossed the street and headed towards the sliproad. With a bit of luck she'd be in the city by morning.